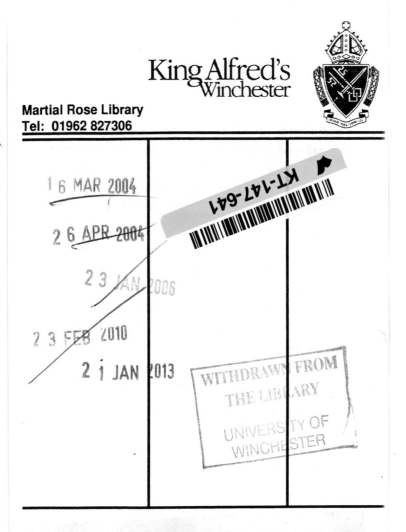

OXFORD BOOKWORMS LIBRARY

Crime & Mystery

Deadlock

Stage 5 (1800 headwords)

Series Editor: Jennifer Bassett
Founder Editor: Tricia Hedge
Activities Editors: Jennifer Bassett and Alison Baxter

SARA PARETSKY

Deadlock

Retold by
Rowena Akinyemi

OXFORD UNIVERSITY PRESS
2000

Oxford University Press
Great Clarendon Street, Oxford OX2 6DP

Oxford New York

Athens Auckland Bangkok Bogotá Buenos Aires Calcutta Cape Town
Chennai Dar es Salaam Delhi Florence Hong Kong Istanbul Karachi
Kuala Lumpur Madrid Melbourne Mexico City Mumbai Nairobi
Paris São Paulo Shanghai Singapore Taipei Tokyo Toronto Warsaw
and associated companies in
Berlin Ibadan

OXFORD and OXFORD ENGLISH
are trade marks of Oxford University Press

ISBN 0 19 4230627

Illustrated by Stephen Player

Typeset by Wyvern Typesetting Ltd, Bristol
Printed in Spain by Unigraf s.l.

CONTENTS

1
Death of a hockey player

More than a thousand people attended Boom Boom's funeral. Many of them were supporters of the Black Hawks ice hockey team. Boom Boom, one of ice hockey's biggest stars, was a player with the Black Hawks until he shattered his left ankle three years earlier. For a long time he refused to believe that he wasn't going to skate again. But in the end he accepted medical opinion and got a job with the Eudora Grain Company. It was Clayton Phillips, Eudora's vice-president, who found Boom Boom's body floating close to the wharf last Tuesday.

Boom Boom's father and mine were brothers, and we'd grown up together in South Chicago, closer than many brothers and sisters. His real name was Bernard, but his childhood friends had called him Boom Boom and the name followed him from childhood into his days with the Black Hawks and beyond. He loved the name and everyone used it.

I was out of town when Boom Boom died, and by the time the police managed to contact me, the funeral had already been arranged by our Polish relations. Boom Boom had made me his executor, but I knew he wouldn't care how he was buried so I didn't argue with the arrangements.

After the funeral, Lieutenant Bobby Mallory fought through the crowd to me, wearing his police uniform. My father had worked for the Chicago police and he and Bobby had been good friends.

'I was sorry about Boom Boom, Vic. I know how much you

two cared about each other.'

'Thanks, Bobby.' A cool April wind made me feel cold in my wool suit. I wished I'd worn a coat. 'Are you going to the party? May I ride with you?'

Bobby agreed, and helped me into the back seat of his police car.

'Bobby, I couldn't get any information from the Eudora Grain Company when I phoned. How did Boom Boom die?'

Bobby frowned. 'I know you think you're tough, Vic, but do you really need to know the details?'

'I just want to know what happened to my cousin. He was young, strong; it's hard to imagine him falling into the water like that.'

Bobby's expression softened. 'You're not thinking he drowned himself, are you?'

I moved my hands uncertainly. 'He left an urgent message for me on my telephone answering machine. I wondered if he was feeling desperate about something.'

'I suppose you'll go on asking questions until you get an answer.' Bobby paused. 'A ship was tied up at the wharf and Boom Boom went under as she pulled away. His body was badly chewed up. It was a wet day, and that's an old wooden wharf – very slippery in the rain. I think he slipped and fell in. I don't think he jumped.'

We stopped in front of Aunt Helen's tidy brick house. The next two hours were difficult for me. The small house filled with cigarette smoke, with the smell of Polish cooking, with the noise of children. Some of my relations told me it was a pity I didn't have a family to keep me busy. Others told me I should go and help in the kitchen.

Boom Boom's grandmother, aged eighty-two, fat and dressed in shiny black, caught my arm. She told me that Boom Boom had been in trouble at Eudora Grain. 'People are saying he stole some papers from his boss,' she said.

My eyes burned. 'It's not true! Boom Boom never stole anything in his life, even when he was poor.'

Grandma stared at me with watery blue eyes. 'Well, that's what people are saying,' she repeated. 'They're saying he threw himself under the ship so that he wouldn't be arrested.'

I shook my head and pushed my way to the front door. I went out into the cold spring air. While I looked doubtfully along the street, wondering whether I could find a cab, a young woman joined me. She was small, with dark hair falling straight just below her ears, and gold-coloured eyes. She wore a fashionable grey silk suit, and I thought I'd seen her somewhere before.

'You're Boom Boom's cousin, aren't you?' she asked with a quick smile. 'I'm Paige Carrington.'

'I thought I recognized you. I've seen you dance a few times.' Carrington was a dancer with the Windy City Ballet.

She gave the triangular smile audiences loved. 'I'd been seeing a lot of your cousin the last few months. I think we were in love. I wanted to meet you. Boom Boom talked about you all the time. He loved you very much.'

'Yes. I hadn't seen him for some months . . . Are you driving back to the city? Can I beg a ride?'

'Of course.'

I followed Paige Carrington down the street. She drove a silver Audi 5000. Either the Windy City Ballet paid extraordinarily well, or she came from a wealthy family.

She didn't say much on the drive back to town. I was quiet

too, thinking about my cousin. I wished I'd seen more of him during the past few months.

Paige dropped me at my office. 'You're Boom Boom's executor, aren't you?' she asked.

I nodded.

'I'd like to go to his place and get some things I left there. I don't have a key.'

'Sure. I was planning to go there tomorrow afternoon to look at his papers. Want to meet me there at two?'

'Thanks. You're sweet . . . Do you mind if I call you Vic? Boom Boom talked about you so much that I feel I already know you. And you must call me Paige.'

My meeting with Boom Boom's lawyer was short, and I drove my Mercury Lynx over to Boom Boom's apartment soon after twelve o'clock. The Black Hawks had paid Boom Boom a lot of money to play hockey, and he'd paid over a quarter of a million for an apartment in a big glass building on Lake Shore Drive with a fantastic view of Lake Michigan.

I opened the door of the apartment and went through the hall into the living room, my feet soundless on the thick carpet. I looked at the view through the big window, and then realized that I could hear something moving. I wasn't alone in the apartment. I looked around the room for a weapon and picked up a heavy gold trophy from a magazine table. I moved cautiously down the hall to the other rooms. The door of Boom Boom's study was open.

Her back to me, Paige Carrington sat at Boom Boom's desk, looking through some papers. I felt both silly and angry. Quietly, I returned to the living room and put the trophy back

4

on the magazine table. Then I went back to the study.

'Early, aren't you? How did you get in?'

Paige jumped in the chair and her face flooded with red. 'Oh! I wasn't expecting you until two.'

'I thought you didn't have a key.'

'Please don't get angry, Vic. I have to be at the theatre at two, so I persuaded the watchman to come up and let me in. I wanted

Her back to me, Paige Carrington sat at Boom Boom's desk.

5

to find some letters I wrote to Boom Boom. They're terribly, terribly personal and I don't want anyone to see them.'

'Find anything?' I asked.

'I've only been through two drawers, and there are six others with papers in them.'

I sat on the desk. 'I have to examine everything, so why don't you leave it to me? I promise you that if I see any personal letters I won't read them – I'll put them in an envelope for you.'

She nodded. 'I brought a suitcase with me. I'll pack up the clothes I left here and leave.'

She went into the bedroom and I looked around the study. Every wall was covered with hockey photographs. In the middle of one wall, looking odd among the hockey players, was a photo of me, taken years ago when I was at the University of Chicago.

I turned back to the desk. There were some sports magazines on it, and a newspaper called *Grain News*, filled with information about the grain business, and interesting, I suppose, if grain was important to you.

'Is that something special?' Paige came back into the room with her suitcase.

I hesitated. 'I've been wondering if Boom Boom jumped under the ship deliberately; but if he was reading a newspaper about grain, then maybe he had become really involved and happy with his job at Eudora Grain.'

'I think Boom Boom was happier after he met me.'

'If that's true, then I'm pleased.'

Her eyes widened. '*If* that's true? Explain what you mean!'

'When I last saw Boom Boom in January, he was still depressed about his ankle. If your friendship helped him, then

I'm glad . . . Did he tell you why he wanted to talk to me?'

She stared. 'Was he trying to contact you?'

'He left an urgent message for me on my answering machine but he didn't say what it was about. I wondered if he wanted my professional help because of trouble at Eudora Grain.'

She shook her head. 'I don't know. I had dinner with him the day before he died, and he didn't talk about you or about any trouble at Eudora Grain. Look, I must get back to the theatre now. I'm sorry if I upset you earlier.'

I stayed in Boom Boom's apartment all day, going through his papers. I was hoping to find a letter that said: 'Dear Vic, I've been accused of stealing some papers. Please help.' I've been a private detective for six years, and I expect to find secrets in people's desks. But I found no secrets, and no letter to me. I didn't find Paige's letters, either. On my way out of the building, I stopped to talk to the watchman. I explained who I was, and asked him not to let anyone into the apartment unless I was there.

On the way home, I was still wondering about the message Boom Boom left on my answering machine. Finally, I said to myself, 'You're a detective, Vic. If you really want to be sure about Boom Boom, try investigating what happened.'

2
On the waterfront

My North Side apartment is the large, inexpensive top floor of a grey stone building on Halsted. The next morning, I woke up around six to another cold, cloudy day. I put on my running shoes and did eight kilometres around Belmont Harbour and back. I had breakfast, picked up the Lynx from the front of my building, and drove to the Port of Chicago, which covers ten kilometres of the shore of the Calumet River. I got lost trying to find my way past some steel factories and a Ford warehouse, and it was nine-thirty before I found Eudora Grain's regional office.

It was a modern building with wide windows looking out on to the river. A dirty old ship was tied up to the wharf by heavy cables, and a railway ran from the wharf into a huge warehouse to the right of the office building.

Clayton Phillips, Eudora's vice-president, came to meet me. He was in his early forties, with pale brown hair and pale brown eyes, wearing a grey silk summer suit. I disliked him immediately, perhaps because he didn't offer me any sympathy for my cousin's death.

'Maybe you could show me exactly where my cousin went in,' I said.

A cold wind whistled around the river, and grain dust blew up at us. We walked to the end of the wharf.

'Your cousin was probably standing here. It was a wet day. We had to stop loading every few hours and wait for the rain to stop. The wooden wharf is old, and it gets slippery when it's wet. Boom Boom probably slipped and fell in. He did have that bad leg.'

'This isn't the ship that was here the day my cousin died, is it?'

'No, of course not,' Phillips said. 'The *Lucella Wieser* was supposed to be here, but she had an accident; so the *Bertha Krupnik* came up instead of the *Lucella*.'

'Where's the *Bertha* now?'

Phillips shook his head. 'She belongs to the Grafalk Steamship Line. You could ask there.'

'Where is their office? I'd like to ask if anyone on the *Bertha* saw Boom Boom go in.'

'I don't think anyone's going to be able to tell you anything. If anyone had seen your cousin go in, they'd have said something at the time.'

'I have a licence.' I fished my private investigator's licence out of my wallet. 'I've asked a lot of people a lot of questions with this.'

Phillips's wooden expression didn't change, but his face turned red. 'I'll go over with you and introduce you to the right person.'

I followed Phillips down the wharf and around the back of the office, to where his green Alfa sat shining next to a rusty truck. He started the car and turned on to 130th Street. I noticed his hands gripping the steering wheel tightly.

'Why do you feel you have to come with me?' I asked.

He didn't say anything for a few minutes. Finally, he said in his deep, tight voice, 'Who asked you to come down to the Port?'

'No one. Boom Boom was my cousin and I want to find out about his death.'

We drove through the entrance to the main Port. The Port of Chicago offices looked modern and efficient. The Grafalk Steamship Line offices were half-way along the wharf and Phillips was clearly a frequent visitor. He led me through the front office, greeting several people by name. Suddenly, we heard a terrible crash. I felt the floor shake, and then there was the sound of glass breaking and metal screaming. People began running outside.

At the north end of the wharf, a ship had crashed into the side of the wharf. A tall crane at the edge of the wharf turned and slowly fell. In a minute two police cars arrived, and the crowd in front of me moved back to let them through. I jumped to one side to avoid an ambulance, and then followed it quickly and came close to the accident.

The crane and a couple of trucks had been waiting on the wharf, and all three were chewed up by the ship which had broken off large pieces of the concrete wharf. The driver of the crane was trapped in a heap of metal, and the police ran to help. An ugly sight. I turned away and found a man looking at me with bright blue eyes.

'What happened?' I asked.

He shook his head. 'Someone made a mistake, and went full ahead instead of turning the ship. That ship weighs around ten thousand tonnes, and that's the result.'

A tall man with a sun-burned face and white hair pushed past me. 'Excuse me. Out of the way, please.'

'Who's that?' I asked the man with blue eyes.

'That's Niels Grafalk. He owns that heap of metal.'

Niels Grafalk, the man I wanted to see. I didn't think this was the time to ask him about the *Bertha Krupnik*.

'Is this ship the *Bertha Krupnik*?'

'No,' my new friend answered. 'Are you interested in the *Bertha*?'

I hesitated. Looking at the excited crowd around me, I felt that Phillips was right: if anyone had seen Boom Boom's accident, they would have been talking about it.

'Look, it's time for lunch,' my friend said. 'Let me take you to lunch at the private club for owners and officers here.'

I agreed, and as we walked away from the accident, I saw Phillips moving hesitantly through the crowd towards the damaged wharf.

The waiter brought our drinks.

'I'm Mike Sheridan, chief engineer on the *Lucella Wieser*.'

'And I'm V.I. Warshawski, a private investigator.'

'Are you related to Boom Boom Warshawski?'

'I'm his cousin . . . The *Lucella* was across from the *Bertha* when Boom Boom fell under the ship last week, wasn't it?'

Sheridan nodded.

'I've been trying to find someone who might have seen my cousin die.'

Sheridan drank from his glass. 'Boom Boom was coming over to talk to John Bemis, the *Lucella*'s captain, that afternoon. We were supposed to take on grain from the Eudora wharf, but someone put water in our holds and we had to dry them out. Your cousin said he knew something about the accident to our ship. He sounded serious, and of course Bemis wanted to talk to him. You don't know what was on Boom Boom's mind?'

I shook my head. 'That's my problem. I hadn't seen Boom Boom for two or three months before he died. I was worried that he might have – well, he was terribly depressed about his ankle. I'd like to know if anyone on the *Bertha* or the *Lucella* saw him fall.'

Sheridan shook his head. 'It's true we were tied up near, but the *Bertha* lay between us and the wharf. I don't think anyone on the *Lucella* could have seen anything.'

The waiter came back to our table. 'Mr Grafalk would like to invite you and the lady to join him and Mr Phillips at his table.'

Sheridan and I looked at each other in surprise. We followed the waiter to a table in a corner of the room. Grafalk stood up and shook hands. He wore an expensive soft jacket and a white shirt, and looked like a man born with money, a man used to controlling things around him.

'Phillips here told me you were asking some questions. Maybe you can tell me why you're interested in Grafalk Steamship.'

I told Grafalk why I wanted to talk to the men on the *Bertha*.

'At the moment, the *Bertha* is going around the Great Lakes,' Grafalk told me. 'She'll stop at Pittsburgh, then Detroit, then on to Thunder Bay. She won't be back in Chicago for two weeks.'

I thanked Grafalk, but his eyes had turned away from me, to a short man in a grey business suit who had walked up to the table.

'Hello, Martin.'

'Hello, Niels . . . Hi, Sheridan. Niels trying to get you to help with his damaged ship?'

'Hi, Martin,' Sheridan said. 'This is V.I. Warshawski, Boom

Boom's cousin – down here asking us all a few questions about his death.'

Martin Bledsoe was introduced to me as the owner of the Pole Star Line, which included the ship the *Lucella Wieser*. Bledsoe sat down and joined us for lunch.

'Sorry about your ship, Niels. What happened?'

'She ran into the wharf. We'll be investigating, of course.'

I asked Grafalk about his company. It was the oldest and the biggest on the Great Lakes, started in 1838. Grafalk became quite enthusiastic, telling me about some of the great ships.

'Mr Grafalk's a fantastic sailor,' Phillips said. 'He still sails his grandfather's old yacht.'

'What about the Pole Star Line?' I asked Bledsoe. 'Is that an old family company?'

'No. I started it myself, eight years ago,' Bledsoe said. 'Before that, I used to work for Niels.'

'I felt deserted when you decided to compete with me,' Grafalk said lightly. 'By the way, I heard about the trouble on the *Lucella*.'

'The damage was minor, but we don't know who put the water in the holds,' Bledsoe said. 'At least the ship itself wasn't damaged.'

'You do have two smaller ships, don't you?' Grafalk smiled at me. 'We have sixty-three other ships to take the place of my damaged ship. My engineer made a mistake; it was an accident, not something deliberate.'

'I did wonder if this was part of your programme to get rid of your smaller ships,' Bledsoe said.

Grafalk dropped his fork. 'We're satisfied with the engineer's explanation,' he said. 'I do hope you won't have any further

13

I heard glass shatter.

accidents, Martin.'

'I hope so, too,' Bledsoe said politely, picking up his wine glass.

Grafalk turned to me again. 'Martin went to a tough school. That's where he learned to be so self-controlled. Being from a wealthy family, I had an easier time.'

I heard glass shatter. I turned to stare at Bledsoe. He had crushed his wine glass in his hand and blood was pouring on to the tablecloth. As I jumped to my feet to send for a doctor, I saw Grafalk watching Bledsoe with a strange expression on his face, and I wondered why the two men disliked each other so much.

3
Watchman, tell us of the night

Martin Bledsoe went to hospital, Niels Grafalk and Clayton Phillips went back to their offices, and Mike Sheridan drove me across the Port to the *Lucella*.

'Why did Grafalk's remark about Bledsoe's school upset him so much?' I asked bluntly.

'I think Martin left school when he was sixteen. Maybe he doesn't like being reminded of that.'

'That's not really a reason to shatter a wine glass in your hand. Why do they dislike each other so much?'

'Oh, that's easy to explain. Grafalk Steamship Line is the only thing Niels cares about. If you work for him, he thinks you should stay forever. I know: I started work at Grafalk. He was furious when I left. John Bemis, too – the captain of the *Lucella*. But Niels found it impossible to accept Martin's departure, maybe because Martin is such a clever businessman: he knows how to make a profit.'

The *Lucella* was bigger than any of the ships I'd seen that day. Three hundred metres long, her red paint smooth, she was huge. I followed Sheridan up a steel ladder attached to her side.

We met Captain Bemis on the bridge. Through the glass windows on every side we saw the deck below us. Men in yellow jackets were washing out the holds. Captain Bemis was a short man with serious eyes and a calm manner.

'Someone deliberately put water in the holds of the *Lucella*,' Bemis began. 'Young Warshawski wanted to talk to us about it.

I told him we thought the criminal was an angry seaman we'd got rid of a few days ago, but Boom Boom said there was more to it than that. I waited on the bridge until five on Tuesday, hoping to talk to him. Then we got news that he'd died.'

'Did anyone here see him fall?' I asked.

Captain Bemis shook his head. 'I'm sorry, but we didn't even realize there had been an accident; none of our men was on deck when the ambulance came.'

I felt disappointed. It seemed so – so unfair that Boom Boom had slid out of life without one person to see him do it. I tried to concentrate on Captain Bemis and the accident to his ship, but it didn't seem important to me. I felt stupid, rushing around the wharf, playing detective, just to avoid admitting that my cousin was dead.

I asked Mike Sheridan to drive me back to the Eudora Grain Company. I picked up the Lynx and drove home. The next morning I drove to Boom Boom's apartment. I stood again at the huge window and looked at the lake. The water was green, and in the distance a ship moved towards the other side of the lake. I stared for a long time before going to the study.

A horrific sight met me. The papers I had left in eight neat piles were thrown around the room. Drawers were opened. Pictures pulled from the walls. Worst of all, a body lay crumpled on the other side of the desk. The man was dead. I guessed his neck had been broken – I couldn't see any wounds. I lifted the head gently: it was the watchman I had spoken to the night before, when I was leaving the building. I ran to Boom Boom's bathroom.

I drank a glass of water from the tap and my stomach felt calmer. I used the phone in the bedroom to call the police. In the bedroom, too, drawers stood open, with clothes thrown on the floor. Someone had been looking for something. But what?

The police said that it was an ordinary burglary. I argued that nothing valuable had been taken, but they insisted that was because the watchman's death had frightened the burglar. I felt I had sent the old man to his death, by asking him not to let anyone into Boom Boom's apartment. It was true that I didn't

A horrific sight met me.

expect anyone to break into the apartment, but it had happened and I felt responsible.

At last the police finished with me and took the body away. I took a last look round. What had my cousin hidden in his apartment? My mind jumped to Paige Carrington. Love letters? How well had she known Boom Boom, really? I needed to talk to her again.

I drove to the Windy City Ballet, stopping on the way for a sandwich and a Coke. The Ballet was an old building, but inside it had been modernized. Some dancers were practising on the stage, but Paige wasn't there. I went backstage, and no one stopped me. I waited, and a few minutes later, Paige came down the hall from the shower, a white towel wrapped round her head.

'Vic! What are you doing here?'

'Hi, Paige. I came to talk to you. When you're dressed I'll take you out for a coffee.'

Her gold-coloured eyes widened. 'I'm not sure I have time.'

'Then I'll talk to you here.'

She shrugged. 'I'll only be a few minutes.'

The few minutes stretched into forty. At last she appeared in a gold silk shirt and a white skirt. She wore a gold and diamond necklace and her make-up was perfect.

'Sorry to keep you waiting,' she said.

We went out into the cold spring air and ordered coffee at a little coffee shop around the corner.

'What were you looking for in my cousin's apartment?'

'My letters, Vic. I told you that.'

'How did you meet Boom Boom?'

'At a Christmas party. Someone interested in buying shares

19

in the Black Hawks invited some of the players.' Her voice was cold. 'What are you thinking? I don't like these questions.'

'The watchman at Boom Boom's building was killed last night when someone broke into Boom Boom's apartment.'

'The night watchman? Henry? Oh, I'm so sorry. Was anything stolen?'

'Nothing was taken, but they tore the place apart. I can't imagine what they were looking for.'

She shook her head, her eyes troubled. 'I can't, either.' She put her hand on my arm. 'I know it sounds crazy about the letters, but it's true.'

We left after that, and I took myself home. I needed some peace and quiet after all that had happened that day. Over dinner I thought about things I needed to do next. Find out about Paige Carrington's background. Talk to Boom Boom's best friend, a star player with the Black Hawks called Pierre Bouchard. And get back to the Port of Chicago.

4
Learning the business

The next day, after my early morning run, I got dressed in dark blue trousers, a white shirt, and a dark blue jacket. Tough, but attractive. Then I drove down to the Port.

At Eudora Grain, I talked to the men as they came off the wharf for their mid-morning break. None of them had seen my cousin's death. They told me that Phillips and Boom Boom had had a terrible argument that morning about some papers, though no one had actually heard what they said.

I thanked them for their time, and went back to the office manager. I told her that I wanted to go through the personal papers in my cousin's office.

'Mr Phillips is out of the office, but Janet, Mr Warshawski's secretary, will help you.'

Janet was a quiet woman aged about fifty, wearing a simple dress and no make-up. She took me to Boom Boom's office, a small, tidy room with maps of the Lakes covering the walls.

'Can you tell me about Boom Boom's work?' I asked.

'Mr Phillips was training him,' Janet said. 'The idea was that he would be able to take over one of the regional offices in another year or so – probably Buffalo.'

'Did Mr Phillips like that idea?'

'It's hard to tell how Mr Phillips feels about anything. I think he was glad your cousin would be leaving soon. Your cousin was an impatient person and he wanted to do everything faster than Mr Phillips.' She hesitated. 'Mr Phillips seemed worried

21

that if Mr Warshawski got too involved with the shipping contracts, then he might take some of the customers with him, when he moved to Buffalo.'

'So did they argue about the contracts? Or the customers?'

'Well, I'll tell you something. You see, Mr Phillips doesn't like anyone touching the contract files.' She looked over her shoulder, in case Phillips was standing there listening. 'It's silly, because we all have to use those files all day long. But he insists that if we take them out of his secretary's office, we have to write a note. Mr Warshawski refused to do that because he thought it was stupid.' She smiled, an amused smile. 'The week before he died, he took several months of contracts home with him.'

'What did he do with them?'

She shrugged. 'I don't know. But he did go and see Mr Phillips with one or two files.'

'Could I look at the files my cousin took home with him?'

She hesitated. 'Why?'

I looked at her kind face. She had been fond of Boom Boom. 'I'm not satisfied with the story of my cousin's death. He was a hockey player, in spite of his bad ankle. It would take more than a slippery wharf to get him into the lake. I'm wondering if someone pushed him in.'

She looked shocked. 'Why would someone push a nice young man like Mr Warshawski to his death?'

I didn't know, I told her, but it was possible those files might give me a clue. I explained to her that I was a private investigator, and she promised to get me the files while Mr Phillips's secretary was at lunch.

I sat at Boom Boom's desk and looked at his desk diary. His

appointments were uninteresting, but he had drawn a circle round some of the dates. At the front of the diary there was a calendar of 1981 and 1982. Boom Boom had drawn circles round twenty-three days in 1981, and three in 1982. I put the diary in my bag and looked through the rest of the office. But I found nothing personal. Janet appeared with the files, packed in a large envelope.

'Please return them as soon as you can,' she said anxiously.

Interstate 94 back to the city was clear at that time of day, and I got back to my office around one-thirty. I phoned Murray Ryerson, crime reporter for the *Herald-Star*, and an old friend of mine.

'What do you want, Vic? Got anything for me on the murder at your cousin's apartment?'

'Nothing on that yet. But I want some background on Paige Carrington, a dancer with the Windy City Ballet. She was friendly with Boom Boom before he died. She was looking for some love letters at his apartment the other day, and then the watchman was killed while someone was searching the place.'

'Vic, whenever you want information like this, it's the beginning of some big story. Is this murder connected with Boom Boom's death?'

'I don't think so. But someone searched his apartment, and I'd like to know more about Paige.'

'OK, Vic. I'll call you in two or three days.'

I opened Janet's envelope and pulled out the files. There were three: June, July and August, showing Eudora Grain's shipments of grain during those months. Each computer report gave details of date and place of departure, names of carriers, weight of grain, cost, and date and place of arrival. Some showed more than one carrier. For example, I found Thunder Bay to St Catharines on 15 June via Grafalk Steamship Line, cancelled, via Pole Star Line, cancelled, and finally via a third carrier at a different price.

I looked at Boom Boom's diary, and pulled out the contracts that matched the dates in June, July and August which had circles drawn around them. Thirteen shipments on those dates had gone to Grafalk. Pole Star had lost seven shipments to Grafalk, but had got two shipments in August.

I tried phoning Pole Star Line, but no one answered. It was too late to do anything else tonight, so I called a friend, and we went out to dinner and then to watch a film.

5
Grounded

The next day I called Bobby Mallory and asked him about the murder at Boom Boom's apartment.

'We did find a footprint on the papers. A size twelve Arroyo boot.' Bobby paused. 'You're not getting involved in this, are you?'

'I am involved: it happened in my cousin's apartment.'

'Don't fool around with me, Vic,' Bobby said. He didn't like me to get involved in police work, especially murder cases.

'Trouble just follows me, Bobby.'

I photocopied the Eudora Grain shipping contracts, and packed the files back in the envelope. I drove to the Port and dropped the parcel with Janet. As I left the office, I met Phillips.

'What are you doing here?' he demanded.

'Signing up for a water ballet class. How about you?'

His face reddened. 'Still asking questions about your cousin? You're wasting your time. I hope you find that out soon.'

'I'm moving as fast as I can. Water ballet can only help.'

He stared at me angrily and walked over to his green Alfa. I drove along the Calumet River to the *Lucella* and asked for the captain, John Bemis. The ship was enormous, held down by steel cables eight centimetres thick. I looked down at the still water. No one was on the wharf, no one knew I was here. I began to see how Boom Boom could have fallen in unnoticed. I climbed the steel ladder to the deck, where twenty people moved busily around, guiding the grain into the huge holds.

Clouds of grain dust rose above the deck.

No one noticed me at first, but at last someone took me to the bridge. Martin Bledsoe was standing with Captain Bemis, looking down towards the deck.

'Hello, Miss Warshawski.' They turned towards me.

Bledsoe's hand was wrapped in bandages, and I asked how it was. He told me that it was beginning to feel better.

'I have a couple of questions for you, Mr Bledsoe, if you have the time.'

I pulled the photocopies of the shipping contracts from my bag and put them on a table. 'These are Eudora Grain's shipping contracts,' I began. 'I was hoping you'd explain them to me.'

'Well, there's no great secret to them. Look at this one. Three million bushels of grain in Peoria, to be moved to Buffalo. First of all, we offered to carry the grain for four dollars twenty-nine cents a tonne. That was before we had the *Lucella* – we can go well under our old prices now because these big ships are so much cheaper to run. Now, in our business, contracts are made and cancelled routinely. Look at this. Grafalk came in to offer four dollars thirty cents a tonne, but with a promise to get the grain to Buffalo a day earlier.'

'So these records are quite ordinary?'

Bledsoe's grey eyes were intelligent. 'What made you think something might be wrong with them?'

'Boom Boom was particularly interested in these files just before he died. I wondered if the fact that these Pole Star contracts ended up with Grafalk was important.'

Bledsoe looked at the contracts again. 'No. Either they promised earlier delivery, or they offered lower prices.'

'My other question is about some dates this spring. The twenty-third of April is one.'

Bledsoe and Bemis looked at each other. 'That's the date we found water in the *Lucella*'s holds.'

'No further accidents are going to happen on this ship,' Captain Bemis said.

Bledsoe nodded. 'I think I'll come with you this time, John. I want to see the *Lucella* unloaded at St Catharines.'

I picked up my papers. I was getting tired of all the work which didn't lead anywhere. Bledsoe walked down to the deck with me.

'We've finished loading for the day. I feel I owe you an apology, for cutting my hand at lunch yesterday. Can I persuade you to eat dinner with me? There's a good French restaurant about twenty minutes from here.'

I agreed, and we had an enjoyable meal together. Bledsoe told me amusing shipping stories, and I told him about my childhood on Chicago's South Side.

It was ten-thirty when Bledsoe took me back to the *Lucella* to pick up my car. 'Thanks for introducing me to a great new restaurant, Martin. Next time I'll take you to an Italian place on the West Side.'

'Thanks, Vic. I'd like to do that. I'll call you when I get back from St Catharines.'

I drove the Lynx on to 130th Street. The night was clear but the air was cold and I kept the car windows up. I drove along Interstate 94 and back on to the Dan Ryan. I was near the University of Chicago exit when I heard a tearing in the engine. I slammed on the brakes. The car didn't slow. I pushed again. Still nothing. The brakes had failed. I turned the steering wheel to move towards the exit. It turned loosely in my hands. No steering. No brakes.

In the mirror I saw the lights of a truck close behind me. Another truck drove beside me on the right. My car was moving to the right, and I couldn't stop it. My hands trembled and I felt sick. I put my hand on the horn and kept it there. The truck to my right pulled out of my way.

The Lynx was going thirty, slowing down, and the truck behind me was going at least seventy. I couldn't stop. I couldn't do anything.

At the last second, the truck behind me moved to the left. I heard a horrible shattering of glass and metal on metal. A car shot into the lane in front of me and turned over. Metal on metal. Glass shattering on the street. A violent crash. A pool of warm wetness on my arm. Light and noise shattered inside my head. And then quiet.

My head ached. I forced my eyes open, but the light stabbed them. I shut them again.

'You're all right now,' a woman's voice said.

'What happened?' My voice was thin and tired.

'You're in Billings Hospital. I want you to sleep now.'

When I woke up again, I was alone. The pain in my head was still there. My left arm was attached to the ceiling by a pulley. I stared at it dreamily. What had I done to my arm? I remembered. My car. The brakes failing.

A nurse came into the room. 'Oh, you're awake now. That's good. We'll take your temperature.'

'I don't want my temperature taken. I want to see the police.'

She smiled brightly. 'Just put this under your tongue.'

I put my hand on the horn and kept it there.

I began to feel angry. 'Will you kindly get someone to call the police for me?'

'Now calm down. The doctor will be here soon, and she'll tell us if you can start talking to people.'

I shut my eyes. My body was still weak. I went back to sleep.

When I woke for the third time, my mind was clear. I sat up in bed, slowly and painfully. I wanted to go home, and use the phone. Carefully, I took my arm out of the pulley. My shoulder moved, and the pain was so strong that tears ran down my cheeks. I shut my eyes and rested for ten minutes. Then I got out of bed, trying not to move my shoulder. At that moment, the doctor came in.

'Glad to see you're feeling better, Miss Warshawski,' she said dryly.

'I thought I'd go home now, since the nurse won't call the police.'

'You must stay here another day or two. You must keep your shoulder still, so that the tear on the muscles is rested,' the doctor said firmly. 'You hit your head against the door as your car turned over. It's badly cut, and you were unconscious for six hours. You mustn't take risks with your health.'

I sat on the bed. 'But I've got so many people to talk to.'

'I'll bring a phone in and you can make your calls.'

Tears filled my eyes. My head was aching. I lay back on the bed and let the doctor reattach my arm to the pulley. I hated to obey the doctor, but I was glad to be lying down.

The doctor brought a phone to me, and I phoned the Port. But the *Lucella* had already sailed.

6
Drinks with Grafalk

The next day I had a stream of visitors. Lieutenant Bobby Mallory, my old friend from the Chicago police, came – carrying a plant from his wife – to talk to me about the accident. He told me that the truck that came up behind me had hit a car when it moved left to avoid me. The driver of the car was killed and his two passengers were seriously injured.

'They weren't wearing seat belts,' Bobby told me. 'It might have helped. Yours certainly saved your life. We've arrested the truck driver – not a scratch on him, of course.'

'Did you inspect my car?'

He looked at me curiously. 'Someone had emptied all the brake fluid. And cut through the steering cable . . . Now who would do a thing like that? Where had you parked your car?'

I told him. He shook his head. 'A lot of vandals down in the Port. You're lucky you got out of this alive. Why can't you stay home and get a husband and some kids?'

Someone brought in an enormous armful of spring flowers. They were from Paige Carrington. Murray Ryerson, crime reporter, came himself. Murray is a big guy with thick reddish hair and a loud voice.

'Vic! Tell me about your accident.'

'Is this a visit or an interview?' I asked crossly. Murray and I have been friends for several years, but our relationship never develops because we are always competing in our work.

'How about an interview as payment for the story on Paige Carrington?'

I brightened up considerably. 'What did you find out?'

'Ms Carrington has one older sister. Mother lives in Park Forest South. Her family doesn't have a lot of money, but she lives in an apartment on Astor Place. She may have a rich friend helping her out. There was some talk about her and Boom Boom the month before he died. But the other hockey players thought she was running after him – he wasn't so interested.'

I felt a stab of pleasure at that. Perhaps I was jealous of Boom Boom's love for the perfect Paige.

'You talk now.' Murray's eyes were bright with interest.

I told him everything I knew about the accident.

'Vandals? I don't believe it. You got someone mad and they cut your steering cable. Someone at the Port. Someone connected with Boom Boom. I'm going to follow you around, Vic. I want to see this happening before it happens.'

'Murray, you get out of here before I ask the nurse to throw you out.'

He laughed. 'Get well soon, Vic. I'd miss you if you didn't . . .'

I drank some water and slept for a while. When I woke up, a young man was sitting in the visitor's chair watching me with an expression of concern on his smooth, round face. It was Boom Boom's friend, Pierre Bouchard.

'Pierre! How nice to see you.'

He smiled. 'I've just seen the story of your accident in the paper. I'm so sorry, Vic. First Boom Boom, and now this.'

I smiled. 'My shoulder will get better.'

'I've come with a message from Boom Boom.' Pierre paused.

'I've been playing hockey in Quebec for two weeks, and when I got back last night there was a letter from him! He mailed it the day before he died.' He pulled a letter from the pocket of his jacket and passed it to me.

Pierre,
I thought I saw Howard the other day in a very odd place. I tried calling him, but his wife said he was in Quebec with you. Give me a ring when you get back and let me know.
Boom Boom

'Who's Howard? Howard Mattingly?'

Pierre nodded. Mattingly was another ice hockey player with the Black Hawks, though not on the first team. Boom Boom never liked him – he couldn't even play hockey.

The letter seemed unconnected with the problems I was trying to solve. But it had been important to Boom Boom. He had written the letter on the twenty-sixth. When had he seen Mattingly? The *Lucella*'s holds had been filled with water on the twenty-third. Could Mattingly have been involved in that?

On Monday, the doctor allowed me to leave the hospital and I went back to my apartment. I got out a bottle of Black Label whisky and sat down in the living room with the telephone. I was going to talk to everyone who might have damaged my car and tried to kill me. My anger had disappeared as my shoulder had got better, but I was determined to discover the truth about my accident.

Pole Star Line told me the *Lucella* had delivered her grain in Buffalo and was on the way to Erie. The ship wouldn't be back in Chicago until June. I phoned Eudora Grain and got Phillips's address from Janet.

My insurance company had provided me with another car, a Chevette, and I drove up to Lake Bluff. The town is a tiny pocket of wealth, and the houses were huge, with beautiful gardens. The weak spring sun shone on trees which were just showing their first pale green leaves.

The Phillipses lived in a house on the shore of Lake Michigan, with a three-car garage. A woman in her early forties answered the door. She was wearing a simple dress which probably cost 250 dollars. Her make-up was perfect, and diamonds hung from her ears.

'Good afternoon, Mrs Phillips. I'm Ellen Edwards with Tri-State Research. We're interviewing wives of important businessmen and I wanted to talk to you. Do you have a few minutes?'

'Is this going to appear in a newspaper?'

'Oh no. We're talking to five hundred women, and no names will be used.'

She agreed, and I asked her a few questions. They had lived in Lake Bluff for five years. Before that they lived in Park Forest South which was much closer to the Port. Lake Bluff was a wonderful place to live. They could sail on the lake and play tennis at the Maritime Club.

'Let's take a normal day and go through it – say last Thursday. What time did you get up?'

I heard all the details of her life. The hours at the tennis club, the shops. At last she gave me the information I'd come for: Clayton hadn't got home that night until after nine o'clock.

'Well, thank you for your time, Mrs Phillips. We'll mail you a copy of the report when we complete it.'

As I said goodbye, I asked who owned the enormous house down the road.

'That's the Grafalks. They're terribly wealthy.'

'Do you spend much time with them?'

'Oh well, Clayton sails with Niels sometimes. And they recommended our names to the Maritime Club. But Claire's not very friendly.'

We said goodbye and I drove down the road. I stopped the car outside the Grafalks' house. It was an enormous, red brick house, with a huge garden. Suddenly, a dark blue Ferrari came round the bend, turned in at the gates, and stopped. Niels Grafalk came up to my car before I had time to disappear.

'What are you doing in front of my house, lady detective?'

'Looking at the view.' I started the car, but he put his hand through the window and grabbed my arm. A stab of pain went through my shoulder.

'I want to know why you were spying on my house.'

'I wasn't spying, Mr Grafalk. If I were, I wouldn't stop outside your front door like this. I'd hide myself and you'd never know I was here.'

The anger in his eyes died down and he laughed. 'What are you doing here, then?'

'Passing through. Someone told me you lived here and I wanted to have a look. It's quite a place.'

He looked amused. 'How about a drink?'

We went up to the house. The garden was green with spring and spring flowers provided bursts of colour at the corners of the house.

'My father built the place back in the nineteen twenties. My wife likes it, so I've never changed it.'

We went in through a side door and then to the back of the house, overlooking the lake. The garden went down to a sandy beach.

'Don't you keep your boat here?'

Grafalk laughed. 'The water is too shallow here. I keep my yacht at the harbour in Lake Bluff.'

I sat down and Grafalk brought me a glass of sherry. I tasted it. It was as smooth as liquid gold.

'If you weren't spying on me, you must have been spying on Clayton. What did you find out? We carry a lot of grain for Eudora. I'd like to know if something is wrong with the company.'

I drank some more sherry. 'I don't know about any problems at Eudora Grain. My main concern is that someone tried to kill me last Thursday night.'

'Kill you?' Grafalk's blue eyes widened.

'Someone cut my steering cable when I was parked at the Port, and I was in a serious accident on the Dan Ryan.'

'And you think Clayton might have done it?'

'Well, it's just posible. But why should he? Any more than you, or Martin Bledsoe or Mark Sheridan?'

'You're sure the damage was done at the Port? Could it have been vandals?' Grafalk got up for more drinks.

'I don't think so. Vandals would damage the tyres or break the windows, not cut the steering cable.'

Grafalk poured me some more sherry. 'How much do you know about Martin Bledsoe?'

I stiffened. 'I've met him a few times. Why?'

'He didn't tell you anything about his background at dinner on Thursday?'

I put the expensive glass down. 'Now who's doing the spying, Mr Grafalk?'

He laughed. 'The Port is a small place and news about ship owners travels fast. I knew about your accident, too, but I didn't know someone had deliberately damaged your car.'

'*Now who's doing the spying, Mr Grafalk?*'

37

'Tell me about Bledsoe's background.'

'It's buried deep. I've never told anyone about it, but if someone tried to kill you, then you should know.'

I didn't say anything. Outside, the house threw a long shadow on the beach.

'Martin grew up in Cleveland. He never knew his father and when he was fifteen he ran away and started sailing the Great Lakes. When he was eighteen he began working in our Buffalo office. He was involved with money, and he stole some of it. I wanted to give him another chance, but my father refused, and Martin spent two years in Cantonville prison. My father died before he came out, and Martin came back to work for me.'

'You must think something is seriously wrong to tell me this.'

Grafalk shook his head. 'If there is something wrong at Eudora Grain, it must involve money. I do sometimes wonder where Clayton Phillips gets his money. But I'm afraid I must ask you to leave now, Miss Warshawski. We're expecting visitors and I have things to do before they arrive.'

He showed me to the front door and watched until I went through the gates and drove off. As I left the wealth of Lake Bluff, I felt confused. Grafalk's sherry and Grafalk's story had clearly been provided for a reason. But what?

7
Stowaway

The next morning I phoned Janet at Eudora Grain and asked her to find out how much Phillips earned. Then I phoned Pole Star Line and found out that the *Lucella* would be in Thunder Bay – Canada's westernmost port on Lake Superior – on Thursday and Friday. I wanted to find out if Grafalk's story about Bledsoe was true, and whether the captain or the chief engineer had damaged my car. I wanted to talk to those guys *now*. So I booked a flight from Chicago to Toronto and then on to Thunder Bay that afternoon. I packed jeans and a shirt, and my Smith and Wesson gun, in a small bag and put my wallet in my jeans pocket.

After an hour in Toronto's bright modern airport, I boarded the small plane to Thunder Bay. We arrived at ten p.m. We were a thousand kilometres north of Chicago and it was still winter. I took a cab to the Holiday Inn and slept late after the long flight. My shoulder felt much better in the morning and I ate a good breakfast. I bought a local newspaper which listed the ships in port. The *Lucella* was at Wharf 67, the Manitoba Grain Company.

I took a cab to Wharf 67. The *Lucella*'s red paint shone in the late morning sun. Above her floated a cloud of white smoke. Grain dust. The *Lucella* was loading. I climbed the steel ladder to the main deck. I stopped to look at the men working on the deck and then I climbed up to the bridge. Only Mike Sheridan, the chief engineer, was there. He looked up in surprise when I came in, recognizing me at once.

'Miss Warshawski! Is Captain Bemis expecting you?'

'I don't think so. Is he around? And what about Martin Bledsoe?'

'They're in Thunder Bay this morning. They won't be back until late afternoon. Not until just before we sail, I'm afraid.'

'You're sailing today? Your office said you'd be here tomorrow.'

'No. We got here a day early, and we'll finish loading around four and sail at five, to St Catharines, at the other side of the lakes.'

I rubbed my forehead. 'Do you stop anywhere on the way where I could get off?'

'We stop at the locks at Sault Ste Marie.' Sheridan was getting annoyed. 'If you're thinking of sailing with us, you'll have to ask the captain.' He returned to his papers and I left the bridge.

I went back to the Holiday Inn, repacked my little bag, and had some lunch. I loaded my gun and pushed it in my belt. At three-thirty I went back to Wharf 67 and once more climbed the ladder to the *Lucella*'s main deck.

The grain was loaded and the men were covering the holes in the deck with steel lids. As I watched, I felt the ship begin to shake. The engines had been turned on. I turned to look at the wharf and I thought I saw someone swimming away from the side of the ship. I stared at the water, and finally I saw a figure rise from the water twenty metres away, close to the shore.

When I turned back, Bledsoe was just coming on board. He went towards the bridge without seeing me. I was just going to follow, when I thought I would hide until the ship left the shore.

I moved behind a pile of huge oil drums and sat down on a metal box. After about forty-five minutes, the *Lucella* slowly pulled away from the wharf. I waited until we were a good kilometre or two from land, and then I made my way to the bridge. I checked my gun, my heart beating fast.

Captain Bemis was at the wheel, but he turned when I came in. 'Ah, Miss Warshawski. The chief engineer said you'd appear.' He was serious, but not angry.

'You're a stowaway, Vic.' Bledsoe gave the shadow of a smile. 'We could lock you in the holds until we get to Sault Ste Marie.'

I sat down at the round table. Perhaps these two men were killers, but now that I was here my anxiety disappeared; I felt calm.

The captain gave the wheel to another officer and he and Bledsoe joined me at the table.

'I'm trying to find out if someone on this ship tried to kill me,' I said.

For ten seconds there was no sound in the small room but the distant noise of the engines.

'Explain that, Miss Warshawski.'

'Gladly. Last Thursday night Martin took me out for dinner. I left my car at the Port. While we were gone someone cut the steering cables and emptied the brake fluid. When my car crashed on the Dan Ryan I escaped with minor injuries. An innocent driver was killed, though.'

'My God!' Bledsoe exclaimed. I watched him carefully. He tried to say something else, but no words came out. His surprise looked real, but . . .

The captain looked at me through narrowed eyes. 'Could I

talk to the Chicago police about this?'

'Of course.'

At last, Bledsoe found his voice. 'Why do you think someone on the *Lucella* might be involved?'

'Only a few people knew I was at the Port. Only a few knew my car.'

'There are a lot of vandals down at the Port,' the captain said.

'I see a lot of vandals in my work, and vandals don't have the tools to do that kind of damage . . . Captain, I'm sure that Boom Boom was killed. And a watchman was killed in his apartment. The killer is connected with this ship or with Eudora Grain. You've got a big machine shop here. I'm sure you've got cutting torches—'

'No!' Bemis exploded. 'Mike Sheridan isn't involved in this. We've been sailing together for twenty years.'

'Anyway,' Bledsoe said, 'there's no reason for Mike – or for any of us – to want to kill you.'

I rubbed my forehead tiredly. 'If I knew what my cousin had found out, then I'd know who the killer was. I thought it was connected with those contracts, Martin, but you told me they were perfectly normal. Perhaps it had something to do with the water in your holds?'

'But we all need this ship. Why would we damage it?'

I looked at Bledsoe. 'Someone might be threatening to tell your secret, Martin.'

Bledsoe's face turned white. 'How dare you!'

'Do you have secrets in your past?'

Bledsoe banged the table. 'If I had a secret, who told it to you?'

Grafalk had told me the truth, Bledsoe's anger told me that. 'I'm only guessing,' I said. 'I just wondered why you smashed a wine glass because Grafalk talked about where you went to school.'

'I see.' Bledsoe gave a short laugh.

'Did you tell Sheridan to damage my car while we were at dinner?'

Bledsoe pushed back his chair. 'Ask him yourself!' He left the bridge, banging the door behind him.

Bemis looked at me coldly. 'I won't allow you to disturb my ship.'

My head ached. 'Very well,' I said tightly. 'I won't disturb your ship. I would like to talk to the chief engineer, however.'

Bemis nodded. 'You may question the chief at dinner.'

I went down to the main deck and breathed the afternoon air thankfully. We were well away from the shore and it was quite cold. I collected my bag from behind the oil drums, and pulled out my coat. I walked down the deck and found a little bench. I sat down and looked at the sun shining on the green-black water.

I reached inside my bag for the Smith and Wesson as Bledsoe came up beside me. He looked surprised when he saw the gun. 'Put that away. I came out here to talk to you.' He sat down beside me. 'Did Grafalk tell you about my crime?'

'Yes.'

He nodded to himself. 'I thought so. No one else knows about it, or cares. I was eighteen years old when I stole that money. And for twenty years Grafalk never talked about it. But when I left to start my own company, Niels started telling me I was still a criminal. But he never told anyone else about it. So why did he tell you now?'

It was a good question. 'I was talking to Grafalk about Clayton Phillips. What do you know about Phillips?'

'Not much. His main job is to act as the controller. He should leave the sales to his salesmen but he wants to be involved in all the shipping contracts, and since he doesn't know all the details, he gets left with expensive contracts occasionally. I noticed that when I was with Niels, and I see it now with my own business.'

It didn't sound criminal, just stupid. 'Can Phillips be cheating Eudora? You told me those shipping contracts were perfectly normal.'

Bledsoe looked at me seriously. 'If you want to be sure, you'll have to look at the invoices. The contracts themselves appear fine, but you want to see what Phillips actually paid.'

I rubbed my shoulder which was beginning to hurt.

'Are you getting off in Sault Ste Marie?' Bledsoe asked. 'I'll fly you down to Chicago – my plane is there and I'm planning to get back to the office this week.'

We got up and went down the long deck. The sun had gone and the sky was turning dark. The first stars were coming out. In the city one doesn't see too many stars.

8
Deadlock

At dinner I talked to Sheridan about my accident. The chief engineer agreed that he had cutting torches in the engine room. 'But we don't keep tools under lock and key.'

'Were you in the engine room that night?' I asked.

He looked me straight in the eye. 'Yes, I was. And my first engineer was with me.'

'Not out of each other's sight all evening?'

'Not long enough to damage a car.'

Around ten-thirty, they brought a narrow bed and some blankets into the dining room for me. I climbed under the blankets in my jeans and shirt, put the Smith and Wesson beside me, and went to sleep almost immediately. The cooks woke me before six as they started preparing breakfast.

After breakfast I packed my little bag for a quick departure: Bledsoe told me we'd have about two minutes to climb over the side of the *Lucella* on to the shore before they opened the lock gates and she went on to Lake Huron. I put my wallet into my jeans pocket and put the Smith and Wesson into the bag. Then I put the bag on the deck and went up to the bridge to watch the *Lucella* slide into the lock.

There were four locks closing the seven-metre drop between Lake Superior and Lake Huron. Only one lock, the Poe Lock, was big enough for the three-hundred-metre ships. We were the second ship into the Poe.

Canada's Sault Ste Marie lay on our left, the huge Algoma

45

steel factory on the shore. After forty minutes, Captain Bemis was told by radio to move into the lock. Slowly we moved forward and the enormous wood and steel gates shut behind us. I went with Bledsoe down to the deck.

It takes about fifteen minutes for the lock to empty its seven million plus litres of water into Lake Huron. A few tourists were watching the ships in the locks from the American side. I watched a man with bright red hair pick up a pair of binoculars and look at our ship through them. I walked across the deck to pick up my bag. I was almost there when I was thrown to the ground, the air knocked out of me. I thought at first that someone had hit me. But when I tried to stand up, I realized the deck was shaking underneath me.

The head cook was standing at the edge of the ship, trying to hold on to the steel cables. I watched in horror as she was thrown backwards and fell over the side of the ship. I didn't understand why we were rising again when there was no water to push us up. I felt horribly sick. Bledsoe was standing near me, his face grey.

Sheets of water rushed up between the sides of the ship and the lock. Thirty metres above us the water rushed, before falling on to the deck, knocking me over again. I wanted to shut my eyes, to shut out the disaster, but I couldn't stop staring. A great cry sounded above the noise of the water. The wood tore and the ship broke in two. We fell again into the lock, falling down into the forward gates. Wet grain poured out of the holds, covering everyone with gold mud. The deck moved sharply down and I held on to the steel cables so that I wasn't thrown into the centre. The broken ship lay still.

✳   ✳   ✳

Thirty metres above us the water rushed.

The air was quiet following the explosion. My legs were shaking. I rubbed the aching muscles of my shoulder. Bledsoe still stood next to me, his eyes glassy, his face grey. I wanted to say something to him, but no words came. An explosion. Someone blew up a sixty-thousand-tonne ship. I saw Captain Bemis come down from the bridge.

'Martin. Our ship. What happened?'

'Someone blew up your ship, captain.' The words came from far away. Bemis was looking at me strangely: I realized I had spoken the words.

Bemis shook his head. 'No. Not my ship.'

I started to argue, but I felt too tired. I suddenly remembered the figure swimming away from the ship at Thunder Bay. That was the person who had planted the explosives. I opened my mouth to tell them, then swallowed the words. No one would be able to accept such news at the moment.

'Martin needs some help,' I said. 'Get him to sit down.'

I needed to get away from the crowd on the deck. There was some important information in my mind, somewhere hidden. If I could get away, stay awake . . . I started towards the bridge, to look for my bag. On my way I passed the chief engineer. He was covered with mud and oil. His eyes stared at me in horror.

'How are things below?' I asked.

'Several men dead. Water everywhere. It was a bomb, you know. It must have been set off by radio signal. But why?'

I shook my head, helplessly, but I suddenly remembered the man with bright red hair and a pair of binoculars. Howard Mattingly, the hockey player Boom Boom had seen in an unusual place, had red hair.

I forgot the ache in my shoulder. I needed to find Mattingly.

Before he got away. I turned away from Sheridan and looked for my bag. I didn't want to follow Mattingly without the Smith and Wesson. The bag was gone. Two shirts, a jacket, a pair of jeans, and a three-hundred dollar Smith and Wesson were all lying hidden in fifty thousand tonnes of grain.

It wasn't difficult to get off the *Lucella*. The emergency team were arriving, followed by a television news team. I pushed my way through an enormous crowd of people enjoying the disaster. But Mattingly was not there. I went across the street to a little coffee shop and drank a cup of hot chocolate. I'd had a shock and I needed a hot drink and sugar. Slowly I began to feel better. Mattingly was probably on his way back to Chicago by car, unless he had a private plane waiting for him at Sault Ste Marie's little airport.

I took a cab to the airport. The daily flight for Chicago left in two hours and I booked a seat on it. Sault Ste Marie is even smaller than Thunder Bay. A few private planes, Cessnas and the like, stood at the edge of the field, and I went over to them. A man was lying on his back under a tiny plane.

'Does Martin Bledsoe keep his plane here?'

The man looked up at me. 'It was here. His pilot flew it out about twenty minutes ago. Some guy came along, said Bledsoe wanted Cappy to fly him to Chicago.'

I was too tired to feel anything – surprise, shock, anger. 'Guy have bright red hair?'

'He had red hair all right. Cappy was expecting the guy. Bledsoe phoned last night and told him.'

I went back to the airport building and boarded the plane for Chicago. I thought I would sleep on the flight, but my mind was too busy. Why would Bledsoe put a bomb on his own ship?

That grey face was real. Perhaps Mattingly had used too much explosive. Why had Bledsoe offered to give me a ride on his plane, if Mattingly was going to use it? I didn't understand and I felt bitter. I liked Bledsoe, and last night I had believed him. Had I misjudged his character completely?

9
Dance for a dead hockey player

When I got home, I slept for ten hours. The phone woke me: it was Janet, from Eudora Grain. She had found out Phillips's salary: ninety-two thousand dollars. That was a lot of money – for me or for Janet. But for Phillips? That huge house, the Alfa, expensive schools for the children, expensive dresses for his wife, the Maritime Club . . . He needed more than ninety-two thousand.

I sat up in bed, still feeling tired. I phoned Pierre Bouchard and asked him if he had seen Mattingly.

'That man! I avoid him if I can.'

'Did you go to a Christmas party, where Boom Boom met Paige Carrington?' I asked. 'Someone interested in the Black Hawks gave the party. Do you know who it was?'

'Oh yes. That party was given by a man called Niels Grafalk.'

'I see,' I said weakly. 'Thanks very much, Pierre. Let me know if you hear from Mattingly.'

So Grafalk had given the party where Boom Boom met Paige. I wondered who had taken her to the party.

I got up and drove over to Boom Boom's apartment. I collected his important papers for the lawyer, picked up the gold trophy from the living room and some of the photos from the wall of the study. I looked at the photo of myself, at the University of Chicago, and took it off the wall. I would get someone to clean the apartment, and then it could be sold.

I put the things into the trunk of the Chevette and drove to the Port. Late Saturday afternoon was a strange time to visit the Port of Chicago. No one was working and the huge ships lay sleeping in the water. I rang the bell at Eudora Grain but no one came. From my back pocket I pulled my burglar's picklocks, and a few minutes later I was in Phillips's office.

I went through all the files in his office, looking for invoices to compare with the shipping contracts. But I couldn't find them. Not one. I went through all the files in the other offices. There wasn't an invoice in the place.

I went home and cooked some spaghetti and tomatoes for supper. I phoned Phillips's house but he wasn't in.

'This is V.I. Warshawski,' I told Mrs Phillips. 'Tell him that the president of Eudora Grain will want to know where all the missing invoices are.'

I had a bath and dressed for an evening at the theatre. Then I drove to the Windy City Ballet. It was already ten-thirty, and I had missed most of the programme. I made sure that Paige was, indeed, dancing tonight, then I went into the tiny theatre and watched the last dance. It was complicated, exciting. Afterwards, I went backstage and waited for Paige in the hall. This time I waited fifty minutes before she finally appeared.

'Hello, Paige.'

She looked surprised. 'Hello, Vic. What questions have you come to ask me tonight?'

'I'd like to know who took you to the party where you met Boom Boom.'

'What?'

'Remember Niels Grafalk's Christmas party where you met

Boom Boom? Or have you forgotten that with the rest of the dead past?'

Her eyes burned suddenly dark and her face turned red. Without a word, she lifted her hand to hit me in the face. I caught her wrist and gently pushed her hand to her side.

'Who took you to the party?' I asked again.

She moved angrily down the hall. 'None of your business. Now will you leave the theatre and don't ever come back.'

Sunday morning. I went out to buy the *Herald-Star* and read it over breakfast. I was half-way through my second cup of coffee when I saw the name Mattingly: Mattingly's body had been found last night in Kosciuszko Park. He had been hit by a car and carried to the park to die.

I called Bobby Mallory and asked him about Mattingly.

'You know I don't like you talking about crime with me, Vic. Why are you interested in Mattingly?'

'He played for the Black Hawks, that's all.'

'Well, he was no good. He owed money to everyone he knew. For once, you leave this case to the police.'

I knew I should tell Bobby what I knew about Mattingly, but I wanted to talk to Bledsoe first and find out why Mattingly had flown home in his plane.

I phoned Murray Ryerson at home. 'I'll give you an interview on the *Lucella* disaster,' I told him.

'What do you know about that?' he asked sharply.

'I was there. I watched the whole thing happen. I may even have seen the person who planted the bomb.'

'I don't believe you're calling me about this! What do you want from me, Vic?'

I asked Murray about Mattingly.

'A small-time criminal. No good. Avoided prison. Desperate for money. Out of town before his death.'

'What shoes was he wearing?'

There was silence. 'You're thinking of the footprint in Boom Boom's apartment,' Murray said at last. 'I don't know, but I'll find out.'

There was nothing more I could do until tomorrow. I went outside and got Boom Boom's papers and pictures from the trunk and took them up to my apartment. As I unlocked the door, I dropped everything. The trophy and pictures fell with a crash. The glass over the pictures shattered and I got a box for the pieces of glass. As I took the broken glass from the photo of me, two pieces of paper slid out from behind the picture.

One piece of paper was an invoice from the Grafalk Steamship Line to the Eudora Grain Company, showing loads by ship, date of departure and arrival. The second piece of paper, written in Boom Boom's tiny handwriting, listed six dates when Pole Star had lost contracts to Grafalk.

I poured myself a drink. Boom Boom had called me about his information and had put the papers behind my picture to prevent anyone else from finding them. A stab of pain hit my chest. I missed Boom Boom terribly. I wanted to cry, but no tears would come.

I wondered if it was time to let the police question everyone. The answer to everything lay in Boom Boom's papers. I'd give myself twenty-four more hours, then turn it over to Bobby.

Two pieces of paper slid out from behind the picture.

The next morning I phoned Phillips again. Mrs Phillips said her husband wasn't in and she didn't know when he would be. She sounded afraid.

I sat at my kitchen table and went through the copies of the shipping contracts from Eudora Grain until I found one that matched the invoice I had from Boom Boom. It was for three million bushels of grain going from Chicago to Buffalo on 24 July 1981. The price in the contract with Grafalk was thirty-three cents per bushel. The invoice from Grafalk had charged thirty-five cents. Two cents a bushel on three million bushels. Came to sixty thousand dollars.

Boom Boom's list of six dates when Pole Star lost contracts to Grafalk was even more surprising. On the contracts I had got from Janet, Grafalk was listed as offering the lowest price. But Boom Boom's list showed Pole Star's offer as the lowest.

It was time to get some explanations from these guys. I wished I had the Smith and Wesson, lying at the bottom of the Poe Lock. I put all the papers back into the bag and drove to Eudora Grain. Phillips wasn't there. Not at home and not at the office. I went to Grafalk's office. He wasn't there either.

I walked over to Pole Star. The office manager was busy with phone calls from newspapers about the *Lucella*'s accident. She told me Martin was down at Plymouth Iron and Steel, on the *Gertrude Ruttan*, another sixteen kilometres around the lake to the east.

The streets there were dirty and poor, reminding me of South Chicago where I grew up. I found Bledsoe on the wharf, watching the ship unloading coal on to the great hills of coal on the wharf. It was three days since I'd seen him, and he looked thinner. It was shockingly noticeable – he must have lost four kilos.

'Martin,' I said. 'Good to see you.'

He smiled. 'Vic! How did you find me? Do you want to watch from the ship?' He went to his car and got another hard hat from the trunk for me. We went up on to the 'deck and watched the coal coming up from the holds. Bledsoe was clearly uneasy, and couldn't stand still. He caught me watching him.

'I'm constantly worried about all my ships now,' he said. 'It will be ten months before they can get the *Lucella* out of the Poe Lock.'

'Can you save the ship?'

'Oh yes, I think so. Sheridan's been all over it with the guys who built her. They'll take her out in pieces, back to Toledo, and then put her together again. She should be sailing again in eighteen months.'

'Who pays to repair the lock?'

'I don't know, but I wasn't responsible for that bomb.'

Suddenly we heard a loud whistle and the noise of the machinery stopped.

'What's wrong?' Bledsoe called. 'Why have you stopped?'

Shouts came from inside the hold.

I started down the ladder into the hold and Bledsoe followed. Six or seven men were down there, looking at something in the coal. I pushed past them.

Clayton Phillips was staring up at me.

Clayton Phillips was staring up at me. His body was covered with coal. The pale brown eyes were open. There was blood on his face and a large hole in the left side of his head.

'It's Phillips,' Bledsoe said, his voice tight.

'Yes. We'll have to call the police. You and I have a few questions to discuss, Martin.' I turned to the group of men. 'Don't touch anything. We'll get the police over here.'

Bledsoe followed me up the ladder to the deck and off the ship. We used the Plymouth offices to call the police, and then went outside again.

'Come on, Martin. Explain things to me.'

He looked at me angrily. 'You owe me an explanation. You're the clever detective. You're always around when disasters hit Pole Star.'

'Why did Mattingly fly back to Chicago on your plane?'

'Who's Mattingly?'

'You don't know Mattingly? Then who did you send back to Chicago on your plane?'

'I didn't. Cappy says I phoned from Thunder Bay and told him to fly someone back to Chicago. But I didn't. You clearly know who this guy is, so *you* tell *me* about it.'

I looked at the blue-green water. 'Howard Mattingly played ice hockey for the Chicago Black Hawks. He was killed on Saturday morning, but on Friday he was up at the Poe Lock. He was the guy who flew in your plane back to Chicago. And he was the one who exploded the bomb on the *Lucella* – I watched him do it.'

Bledsoe grabbed my arm in anger. 'Why haven't you told the police? I've been talking for two days and you – you've been hiding this information.'

I pulled my arm away and spoke coldly. 'I only realized later. I didn't recognize Mattingly immediately. And then I found he had gone back to Chicago on your plane and that upset me. I wanted to talk to you about it first, before I told the police. And now I'd like to know where you were yesterday morning, when Phillips went missing.'

His eyes were dark pools of anger in his face. 'How dare

you!' he shouted.

'Martin: listen to me. The police are going to ask that question, and you'll have to answer.'

'I was at the Poe Lock until late yesterday. I only came back to Chicago about ten last night.'

'Where was the *Gertrude Ruttan*?'

'She came into the Port on Saturday afternoon and has been tied up here all weekend.'

'I want to know why you let so many contracts go to Grafalk when you offered a lower price. Why?'

He shook his head impatiently. 'I didn't kill your cousin, Warshawski. If anyone did, it was Grafalk. Why don't you find out how he blew up my ship and forget these contracts?'

'Martin, it seems that you and Grafalk were helping each other on those contracts. Mattingly flew back to Chicago in *your* plane and Phillips's body was found on *your* ship. If I had all that information, I wouldn't look further – if I was a cop.'

'All right. It's true,' he shouted. 'I did let Niels have some of my orders. Are you going to put me in prison for it?'

I didn't say anything.

After a pause, he continued more calmly. 'I was trying to borrow money to buy the *Lucella*. Niels was getting desperate for orders. He couldn't get enough, because of those small ships of his. He told me he would tell the Fort Dearborn Trust about my time in prison if I didn't give him some of my orders.'

'Could that really have hurt you?'

He gave a bitter smile. 'I didn't want to find out. I was trying to borrow fifty million dollars. I couldn't see any bank giving me anything if they knew I'd been in prison for two years for stealing.'

'I see. And then what?'

'Oh, as soon as the *Lucella* was mine I told Niels to tell anyone he wanted. I was making money with the *Lucella* and no one would care about my past. Niels was furious.'

'It's a big jump from getting a few shipping orders to blowing up your ship.'

He insisted that no one else cared enough. We talked about it for half an hour or more, but he wouldn't change his mind. I told him finally that I'd investigate Niels too.

11
A house of mourning

I woke up early the next morning. I ran slowly over to Belmont Harbour and back. I only did three kilometres instead of my normal eight, but the ache returned to my left shoulder. I took a long shower and rubbed some oil into the painful muscles.

I was on the road by nine o'clock. My first stop was the Title Office at City Hall, where owners of all the buildings in Chicago are listed. A clerk showed me a heavy book which listed the owners of buildings in Astor Street. Paige's apartment was owned by the Fort Dearborn Trust. Number 1123785-G.

Curiouser and curiouser. I went out to find a phone. I'd been to Law School with a woman who worked for the Fort Dearborn Trust. I thought I'd call her and remind her that we were friends.

The information was confidential, she told me. She would be thrown out of the bank if she told me. I finally persuaded her that the *Herald-Star* would get the information for me, if she didn't.

'You haven't changed a bit, Vic. I remember how you always persuaded people to do things for you at school.'

I laughed, and she agreed to call me at home that night with the name of the person behind the number.

I then called Murray. 'You've given us a story for the front page tomorrow,' he said.

'What are you talking about?'

'That Arroyo walking boot. Mattingly was wearing them

when he died, and we're sure they match the footprint the police found in Boom Boom's place. Got any other news?'

'No. I was hoping that you might have something for me. Talk to you later.'

I drove through the traffic to the Kennedy Expressway. The weather had finally warmed up a little. Under a clear blue sky, trees along the expressway put out green leaves towards the sun. Off the Kennedy to the Edens, past the painfully tidy houses of the Northwest Side where people spent their salaries with anxious care, through the wealthier suburbs of Lincolnwood and Stokie, on to the Tri-State Expressway and the northern areas of the very rich.

I drove past the Phillips's house and parked the Chevette on the road. Phillips's green Alfa was parked in front of the house, next to a red Monte Carlo. And a silver Audi 5000. The sight of the Audi stopped my heart for a moment.

An older woman answered the door. 'Are you one of Jeannine's friends? She's sitting through here. It's awfully nice of you to visit.' Her eyes reminded me of her daughter, but her dress looked inexpensive.

Jeannine was sitting in the pale blue living room at the back. Her face was carefully made up and it was difficult to see how she felt about her husband's death. Across the room, feet on the chair under her, sat Paige Carrington. She put down her teacup with a crash on a glass coffee table at her left arm.

'Vic! I won't allow it! Are you following me everywhere?'

'I thought I recognized your Audi out there,' I remarked.

'No, you must go away. I'm not answering any questions now,' Jeannine said. 'My – my husband died yesterday.'

Paige turned to her. 'Has she been after you, too?'

'Yes. She was out here last week asking me a lot of questions about my life as a businessman's wife. What was she talking to you about?'

'My private life.' Paige's gold-coloured eyes watched me.

'I didn't follow you here, Paige. I came to see Mrs Phillips. Though I'm curious about who's paying for your apartment. Astor Place – that's got to cost more than eight hundred a month in rent.'

Paige's face turned white under her make-up. 'You must be joking, Vic. If you bother me any further, I'll call the police.'

'I'm not bothering you at all. As I said, I came here to see Mrs Phillips. I'm afraid I'm a detective, Mrs Phillips, and last week I was trying to find out if your husband attempted to murder me two weeks ago.'

Her tightly closed mouth dropped open with surprise.

'Your husband had a lot of money beyond his salary. I'd like to talk to you privately about it. Unless you want your mother and Ms Carrington to hear.'

Tears began to run through the make-up on her cheeks. 'He promised me no one would ever know.'

'What are you talking about?' her mother asked. 'Clayton had a very good salary at Eudora Grain.'

'That's OK, Mother. I'd better talk to this woman.' She turned to Paige and said with sudden bitterness, 'I suppose *you* know all about it.'

Paige gave her triangular smile. 'I know quite a bit of it. Talk to Vic, Jeannine. If you don't, she'll only come in uninvited and search the house for your bank books.' She moved over to Jeannine's chair and kissed the air by her cheek. 'I'll see you at the funeral tomorrow afternoon – unless you want me to come again before then.'

'No, that's all right, dear,' Jeannine's mother said. 'We'll manage.' She left the room behind Paige.

I looked after them puzzled. Those last words sounded too friendly. 'How do you know Paige?' I asked.

Jeannine turned her tearful face to me. 'How do I know her? She's my sister.'

'Your sister!' I sat down. 'Did you take her to the party where she met Boom Boom Warshawski?'

She looked surprised. 'What party was that?'

'Niels Grafalk had a party at Christmas. My cousin Boom Boom went along with some other hockey players. I want to know who took Paige.'

Jeannine swallowed a strange smile. '*That* party. No, we didn't go. If you want to know who Paige went with, though, you ask her.'

I looked at her narrowly. She knew, but she wouldn't tell. 'Tell me about the invoices, Jeannine. I called about them Saturday night. What did your husband do when he got my message?'

She began to cry again, but in the end she told me that when Clayton got the message he made a phone call. He left the house a few minutes later, at about one thirty Sunday morning. That was the last time she ever saw him.

'Now tell me about the invoices. He would write down one price in the Eudora Grain books, but send an invoice at a higher price. Is that right?'

'You don't understand!' She stared at me with angry eyes. 'I hated Park Forest South! I wanted to live in a wealthy part of Chicago, with a bigger house and better neighbours.'

'So your husband's salary wasn't enough for you.'

'He – he didn't do it with all the invoices, only about ten per cent.'

'And then my cousin found out. He was going through the papers, and he compared some invoices with the contract orders.'

'It was terrible,' she gasped. 'He was going to tell the

'You decided to kill my cousin to keep yourself in expensive clothes.'

president of Eudora Grain. It would have been the end of Clayton's job. We would lose the house, the club. It would have been the end of—'

'Stop it,' I said coldly. 'It was a choice between the Maritime Club and my cousin's life.'

She didn't say anything. I took her by the shoulders and I shook her. 'Answer me! You decided to kill my cousin to keep yourself in expensive clothes. Is that what happened? Is it?'

In my anger I had lifted her from her chair and was shaking her. Mrs Carrington came into the room.

'What's happening here?' She took my arm. 'I think you must go now. If you don't leave, I'll call the police.'

Somehow I heard her scratchy voice and forced my anger back. 'You're right. I'm sorry, Mrs Carrington.' I turned to Jeannine. 'Just one more question before I leave you to your mourning. What part did Paige play in all this?'

'Paige?' she whispered, rubbing her shoulders. She gave the secret smile I'd seen earlier. 'Oh, Paige watched Boom Boom. But you'd better talk to her. She hasn't told you my secrets. I won't tell you hers.'

'That's right,' Mrs Carrington said. 'You girls must be good to each other. You only have each other.'

'As well as your expensive homes in Lake Bluff and Astor Place,' I said.

12
A question of money

I was sick by the side of the road as soon as I got out of the house. I walked slowly down the road to the Chevette and sat in it for a long time. My shoulder ached and I felt a sharp pain across my chest every time I breathed. I had found out about Boom Boom's death. My face felt wet. I passed a hand across my eyes, expecting to find blood. I was crying.

After a while I looked at my watch. It was one o'clock. I started the engine and slowly turned the car and drove up the road past the Phillips's house to the Grafalks'.

I climbed the shallow wide steps to the front door and rang the bell.

Mrs Grafalk opened the door. She was dressed to go out, in a pink silk suit. Her eyes were sharp but not unfriendly.

I handed her my card. 'I'm a detective. I want to talk to you about Clayton and Jeannine Phillips.'

An expression of dislike crossed her face. 'I can't tell you much about them. Clayton is – was, I should say – a business friend of my husband's. Clayton helped Niels in some way and Niels introduced them at the Maritime Club because he was grateful. I tried to interest Jeannine in what I do – collecting money for the poor in Waukegan – but she can only think of her clothes. Does that answer your questions? I'm afraid I must go now. I'm on my way to a meeting.'

She came out of the door, moving quickly to the Bentley parked in front.

Slowly driving back to Chicago, I thought about Mrs Grafalk's remarks. How could Clayton have helped Grafalk? Had he given Grafalk some of the money he had stolen from Eudora Grain? But what did Grafalk need a few thousand dollars for? I remembered that Grafalk's ships were all smaller ships, and that the three-hundred-metre ships were more efficient. Suddenly, I saw the whole thing. I even had an idea where Clayton Phillips had been murdered and how his body had been carried on to the *Gertrude Ruttan*.

I parked the Chevette and ate a chicken sandwich at a little bar behind the Ajax Insurance Company building. Then I went into the Ajax building and asked to see the person dealing with the fifty-million-dollar bill Ajax was going to pay for the *Lucella*. Finally, they sent me up to the fifty-third floor, to the Special Risks Department. Roger Ferrant had come over from London to deal with the insurance problems of the *Lucella*.

'I may have some information for you about the accident to the *Lucella*,' I told him.

Roger Ferrant was very tall, with long brown hair falling over his eyes, and he spoke with an English accent. We sat down in chairs near the window.

'I'm investigating the murder of a young man at Eudora Grain,' I went on. 'I was on board the *Lucella* when she blew up, and I'm sure the two crimes are connected. I'd like to ask you some questions. First of all, what's happening to the ships on the Great Lakes since the accident at the Poe Lock? Can ships still get through?'

'Well, ships can still use the other locks,' Ferrant explained, 'but the biggest ships are shut off from the upper lakes for a year – until the Poe is fixed.'

69

'So the smaller ships have an advantage?'

He smiled. 'Until the Poe is fixed.'

'How profitable is the Grafalk Steamship Line?'

He looked at me in surprise. 'Grafalk's is the biggest shipping company on the lakes.'

'I know – but do they make money? Grafalk has only small ships and I understand they are unprofitable.'

Ferrant shook his head. 'All we do is insure the ships. Why do you want to know, Miss Warshawski?'

'There has to be a reason for the bombing of the *Lucella*. I'm trying to find out if that reason was to give the smaller ships an advantage. Grafalk is profiting from this accident. I want to know how successful his business is.'

Ferrant looked amused. 'You certainly look for the less pleasant side of human nature . . . I'll get the files.'

He asked his secretary to bring him five years of Grafalk Steamship files and after a few minutes a middle-aged woman in a smart business suit came into the office with a pile of files.

Ferrant was suddenly enthusiastic. 'Now we'll see the whole picture: workers' insurance and cargo insurance as well as the ship insurance which I deal with. You go through the workers' insurance files and find out how many people sail for him every year. Then we can guess his costs. I'll go through the cargo insurance files and see how much he's earning.'

I sat down at a round wooden table and began going through the files. We worked through the day, and it became clear that each year it cost Grafalk about a hundred and twenty million dollars to run the Steamship Line; and that for the last five years his ships had made no more than a hundred million dollars a year.

'That answers your question all right,' Ferrant said. 'Grafalk is definitely losing money.' He closed the file in front of him.

'Where's Grafalk been getting the money to pay the Steamship bills?' I asked.

'He has a profitable railway that connects the Port of Buffalo with Baltimore. And he owns a computer company. He must have used profits from those businesses to help the Steamship Line.'

I asked Ferrant if I could use the phone. My answering machine told me that the woman at the Fort Dearborn Trust had left a message that I could call her at home.

'Hello, Vic. I got the information you wanted.'

'I hope you've not lost your job.'

She gave a little laugh. 'No – but you owe me some free detective work. Anyway, the building is owned by a Niels Grafalk – Vic. Are you there? Hello?'

'Thanks, Adrienne,' I said mechanically. 'Let me know when you need the detective work.'

Ferrant looked at me politely. 'Something wrong?'

'Nothing I hadn't suspected since this morning. But it's upsetting anyway – Grafalk owns buildings as well as everything else.'

'You know, Miss Warshawski, you're being terribly mysterious. Would you mind telling me what's going on?'

'Some other time. There's someone I need to talk to. I'm sorry, but I must go.'

I left and drove to Astor Place, a huge pink brick building. I rang the bell to Paige's apartment, and when her voice came through on the house phone I said it was Jeannine and she told me to come in.

71

Paige was waiting at the top of the stairs.

'What brings you to the city, Jeannine?' she was saying as my head came into sight. She stopped in surprise for a second too long. I reached the door before she started to shut it and pushed my way inside her apartment.

'We're going to talk, Paige.'

'I have nothing to say to you. Get out of here before I call the police.'

I sat down and looked around the large, light room. Expensive gold curtains hung at the windows. 'The police will be very interested in your part in Boom Boom's death. Please do call them.'

'They think it's an accident.'

'But do you, dear Paige? Do you think it was?'

She turned her face away, biting her lip.

'Jeannine told me this morning you were watching my cousin. I thought she meant for her and Clayton. But she wasn't talking about them, was she? No. You were watching him for Grafalk.'

She didn't say anything.

'How long have you been Grafalk's mistress?'

Colour stained her cheeks. 'What an offensive remark. I have nothing to say to you.'

'Then I'll have to do all the talking. You tell me if I'm wrong. Niels knew that Clayton was cheating Eudora Grain. He promised to keep quiet if Clayton gave Grafalk more shipping orders.'

'I don't know anything about the Grafalk Steamship Line. I've only met Niels Grafalk at my sister's house.'

'Oh, nonsense, Paige. Grafalk owns this building.'

'How do you know that?' she demanded. 'Did Jeannine tell you?'

'No, Paige. Your sister kept your secret. But names of property owners are public in Chicago. Now tell me why you watched Boom Boom for Niels?'

'Vic, I had no choice. Niels pays for everything. This place, all the furniture. My bills. My clothes. I owe him so much. It seemed easy to go out with your cousin a few times and see if he had learned anything about the Eudora Grain invoices. I liked Boom Boom, Vic. When I told Niels that Boom Boom had found out the truth, he wanted Clayton to get rid of Boom Boom immediately. But I told him not to.' She lifted her chin and looked at me proudly. 'We went sailing on that Saturday and Niels tried to persuade Boom Boom to keep quiet. On Monday, Clayton had a terrible row with Boom Boom. But then – then he slipped and fell. That accident was a good thing. I was afraid Niels might do something desperate.'

I was silent. I couldn't find words that matched my horror and anger. Finally I whispered, 'What about Clayton? Were you with Niels Sunday morning when he put a big hole in the side of Clayton's head?'

She looked at me with gentle blame. 'I don't think you should talk to me like that, Vic. You may not like Niels, but he is my lover.'

I gave a burst of mad laughter. 'Why should I care about you and Grafalk? It's what the two of you did to my cousin that I care about.'

Paige looked at her watch. 'Yes, well, I've told you how much I owe Niels. He's coming over in a few minutes, too, so unless you want to meet him I suggest you leave.'

I got up. 'There never were any love letters, were there? It was the copy of Grafalk's invoice you were looking for in Boom Boom's apartment the day after the funeral, wasn't it? If it was, I've found it.'

13
The fire ship

Back outside I sat on the steps, unable to move any further. The day had started out at Jeannine's with the fact that her husband had pushed Boom Boom under the *Bertha Krupnik*. Now came the news that Paige had gone out with Boom Boom only to spy on him for Grafalk. What good would it do Boom Boom if I could prove Grafalk had ordered his death? Revenge brings only limited pleasure. The one thing I might be able to prove was that Grafalk murdered Phillips. I knew the cops wouldn't believe Grafalk was a murderer without proof. But if I could find a witness, someone who saw Grafalk and Phillips on his boat Sunday morning – or if there were some bloodstains on Grafalk's boat . . .

I stood up and went to my car. At home I put some plastic bags in my pocket and a small knife to cut up a piece of deck or carpet with blood on it. Then I went out to the car and drove to the lake. Instead of turning south on Green Bay for Lake Bluff, I went on to Sheridan Road and turned left, following the road up to the harbour.

A guard was on duty at the entrance. I gave him a bright smile. 'I'm Niels Grafalk's niece. He's expecting me to join a party on his yacht.'

'Down to the wharf, then turn left. You can't miss it – it's the biggest boat there.'

I followed the road down to the lake. It was nearly six, and the sun was low in the sky. Grafalk's yacht was beautiful, in the golden light of spring. Painted white and green, she floated easily against the ropes that held her to the wharf, like a beautiful sea bird.

I parked the Chevette and walked out to the boat. I pulled myself on to the deck and began to examine the deck, on hands and knees, like a real detective. I found two short pale brown hairs caught in the deck at the top of the ladder. I pulled out the hairs and put them in a little plastic bag. Then I went downstairs.

The door was locked and it took me a few minutes to force it open. There were several bedrooms and a kitchen and bathroom, but I didn't think Grafalk and Phillips would have fought in there. I went into the sitting room. I noticed that in front of the small electric fire, the thick green carpet looked a different colour. I went over and knelt down near it: the carpet was wet and there was a strong smell of cleaner, but there was no blood. I found another hair. Perhaps the police with their equipment would be able to find blood.

With my knife, I cut a small piece of carpet from the place where I'd found the hair. As I put the piece into another plastic bag, I heard a noise on the deck. Then footsteps. Someone had come on to the boat. I put the plastic bag into my pocket. Holding the knife firmly, I went to the door. I heard the sound of voices, and then the engine started and the boat began moving slowly backwards.

I looked around for a hiding place. There was none. Finally, I heard a footstep on the stairs.

'Miss Warshawski, I know you're there. I saw your car on the wharf.' It was Grafalk.

My stomach turned over. I felt too weak to speak. I breathed

'Do sit down, Miss Warshawski.'

slowly and stepped out of the door.

'Good evening, Mr Grafalk.' My voice didn't shake and I
was pleased with myself.

'I think we can talk more easily down here,' Grafalk said.
'Sandy will be able to manage the boat alone for a while.' He
took my arm and moved me back into the sitting room. 'Do sit
down, Miss Warshawski. You know, by now you should be

77

dead several times. You're a survivor. And your discoveries, as I learned from Paige, are really very accurate.'

I sat down in one of the chairs near the table. 'Thank you, Mr Grafalk.'

Grafalk opened the drinks cupboard. 'A drink, Vic? You don't mind if I call you that, do you?' He sat down opposite and poured himself a glass of whisky. There was an expression of excitement on his face. 'By the way, who are you working for? Not Martin, I hope.'

'I'm working for my cousin.'

'Revenge. I see. Paige says you don't believe Boom Boom's death was an accident.'

'You told Phillips to kill my cousin. You told Mattingly to search Boom Boom's apartment, and he killed the night watchman. You told Phillips to damage my car, and I was nearly killed. You told Mattingly to blow up the *Lucella*, and then you killed Mattingly. Oh yes. And then you killed Phillips.'

Grafalk poured himself some more whisky. 'Mattingly did most of the damage, and he's dead. Right now, the police seem extremely uninterested in me.'

'When they have the proof that Phillips received his head wound here, their interest will catch fire.'

'Yes, but who's going to tell them? I won't. And you, I'm afraid, aren't going to be with us when we return to harbour. So you won't.'

He was trying to frighten me and succeeding very well. 'Phillips called you Saturday night after he got my message, didn't he?' I asked.

'Yes. I'm afraid Clayton was breaking down. He was clever enough, but he worried about details too much. He knew that

78

if you told the president of Eudora about the invoices, his job would be finished.'

'Why did you kill him, though? You own the Steamship Line – how could it harm you if the public discovered you cheated Eudora Grain? You can't lose your job.'

'Oh, I agree. Unfortunately, Clayton knew my feelings towards Martin too well. He suspected I was responsible for the accident to the *Lucella*, and he threatened to tell the police if I didn't help him with the president of Eudora.'

'So you put a hole in his head and sailed him down to the Port. Putting him on one of Bledsoe's ships was a clever idea.'

Grafalk was annoyed that I had guessed so easily. 'I won't take those risks with you, Vic. I'll leave you a couple of kilometres from shore, with a good strong weight to hold you down.'

I have always been afraid of death by drowning more than any other end – the deep water pulling me down into itself. My hands were trembling a little. I pushed them against my legs so that Grafalk couldn't see.

'I didn't realize how much you hated Bledsoe. You threatened him while he was trying to borrow money to buy the *Lucella*, but once he'd got the ship he stopped giving you contracts. That's when you got Mattingly to put water in the *Lucella*'s holds.'

Grafalk wasn't so calm now. 'How'd you know that?' he asked sharply.

'Boom Boom saw Mattingly at the Port . . . But what I really want to know is how long the Grafalk Steamship Line has been losing money?'

He got up with a sudden movement that knocked his whisky

glass over. 'Who told you that?'

'Niels, it's obvious. Grafalk Steamship is the only thing you really care about. Your argument with Bledsoe at lunch, my first day at the Port, was about getting rid of your unprofitable old ships.'

He pushed the bottle of whisky from the table with a violent movement and sent it flying against the wall. It broke and a shower of glass and whisky hit my back.

'I never thought the new ships would be profitable,' he shouted. 'They're too big. There weren't many ports that could take them. I was sure they wouldn't succeed.' His face was angry. 'But then I started losing orders. And Martin! I saved him from prison. I gave him his old life back. And how did he thank me? By building that *Lucella Wieser* right under my nose.'

'Why didn't you build your own?'

'I couldn't afford to. My other businesses were paying the Steamship bills, and I was losing so much money that I couldn't find anyone to lend me more. I wished I could blow up all my ships and collect the insurance. Then I had a better idea. Get rid of the *Lucella* and close the upper lakes to the bigger ships at the same time. I can't keep the Poe Lock shut forever, but I can make enough money in the next twelve months to start building some new ships next year. And Martin should be finished by then.' He laughed crazily.

'I see.' I felt tired and miserable. I couldn't think of any way to stop him.

The anger had disappeared from Grafalk's face and the expression of excitement returned. 'And now, Vic, I want you to come on deck with me.'

I pulled my knife from my pocket. Grafalk smiled at it.

'Don't make it difficult for yourself, Vic. I'll kill you before you go overboard – no unpleasant drowning for you.'

My heart was beating fast but my hands were calm. Grafalk started around the table for me. I let him follow until my back was to the door. I turned and ran down the hall, cutting through my shirt with the knife as I ran. I cut my arm and blood rolled down it to my hand.

In the dining room I kicked over a cupboard with glasses in it. The cupboard crashed to the floor. I ran behind the table and wiped my bleeding arm on the curtains.

'What are you doing?' Grafalk shouted.

'Leaving something for the police,' I gasped. I drew the knife across the table and then began to cut the chairs. Grafalk stood still for a moment and then came forward again. I slid a chair in his path and turned into the kitchen.

The gas cooker stood there and a mad idea grabbed me. I turned the cooker on and a blue flame shot up. As Grafalk came through the door at me I tore a curtain down and dropped it on the flame. It caught fire immediately. I waved the curtain around like a torch and the other curtains caught fire.

Grafalk dived at me and I jumped out of the way. He fell, heavily, and I ran with my torch back to the dining room where I set the curtains on fire. Grafalk ran after me with a fire extinguisher which he directed at the curtains. I ran back down the hall and up the stairs to the deck. Grafalk ran behind me. 'Stop her, Sandy! Stop her!'

A sandy-haired man at the wheel looked up. I ran to the back of the boat. It was dark now and the water was black. Lights from other boats shone far away and I screamed hopelessly for help.

Grafalk ran on to the deck towards me, a mad expression on his face, the fire extinguisher held in front of him. I breathed deeply and jumped overboard. The water was very cold. For a minute, thinking of the deep water stretching beneath me, terror held me. I forced myself to breathe deeply, to stay calm. I kicked off my shoes, then reached into the water and pulled off my socks and shirt. The yacht, its sails up, was moving at a good speed and had gone some nine metres past me.

I was alone in the icy river. I might last twenty minutes – not enough time to swim to shore. My left shoulder ached from the cold. The yacht started to turn. Swimming on my back, I saw Grafalk on the deck. I was close enough to see his white hair and the gun in his hand.

Something exploded – probably the gas in the kitchen – and a small fireball flew up and landed on the deck. Sandy appeared next to Grafalk and jumped into the water. Grafalk shook his arms in anger. His gun in his hand, he searched the water for me and found me. He pointed the gun and stood there for a long minute. I was too frozen to do anything except move my legs mechanically up and down.

Suddenly he dropped the gun over the side and raised his right arm in a greeting to me. Slowly he walked towards the fire behind him. And then the yacht exploded.

14
The long goodbye

We sat outside, looking at Lake Michigan. The water, blue under a soft summer sky, moved gently over the sand below us. The May day was bright and clear, although the air was cool out of the sun.

Claire Grafalk was wearing a grey dress and a heavy pearl necklace. She poured me a glass of wine. 'Now. I must hear what happened. The papers gave only a few details. What happened to Niels's boat?'

'There was an accident in the kitchen and the ship caught fire.' This was the answer I had given to the police and to Murray Ryerson, after a passing boat had rescued me from the icy water, and I wasn't going to change it now.

Mrs Grafalk shook her head forcefully. 'No, my dear. That won't do. The president of Ajax Insurance Company came to visit me two days ago with an extraordinary story. That Grafalk Steamship was losing money and you suspected Niels had blown up Martin's ship.'

I put the wine glass down. 'And what do you want me to tell you?'

She looked at me sharply. 'The truth. I still have to deal with this matter. I shall have to do something with the Grafalk Steamship Line. Martin Bledsoe would be the best person to have the company now. But I must know the whole story before I talk to him or to my lawyers.'

'I don't have any proof. Wouldn't you prefer to let the dead bury the dead?'

'Miss Warshawski. For more than ten years Niels and I have lived separate lives. Neither of our children were interested in Grafalk Steamship and Niels couldn't think of anything else. During the past eight or nine months, Niels was growing more and more peculiar. I want to know why you were on Niels's boat and how it came to burn up.'

'I would have liked to see her mourn.'

I drank some more wine. If anyone had the right to know, Claire Grafalk did. I told her the whole story, beginning with Boom Boom's death and ending with the icy waters of Lake Michigan.

'And the proof of Clayton's death?'

I shook my head. 'I still have the plastic bags. But I don't want to use them. There's no one left for the police to deal with. I don't think the government will be able to prove that Niels blew up the *Lucella*.'

Claire looked away from me and said in a flat voice, 'Niels left Paige Carrington a building on Astor Place.'

I breathed deeply. Paige was the place that still hurt, the pain in the chest every time I thought of her.

Mrs Grafalk still didn't look at me. 'She's in London now, with another wealthy ship owner.'

'Do you mind so much?' I asked gently.

Tears shone in her bright eyes, but she gave a trembling smile. 'Do I mind? Niels has been dead to me for many years. But once – it was different. Because of the man I once loved, I would have liked to see her mourn.'

GLOSSARY

apartment *(American English)* a flat; a set of rooms in a large
  building
ballet a special kind of dancing with music, which usually tells a
  story
binoculars a pair of glasses which makes distant objects seem
  nearer
break *(n)* an interval during work for lunch, coffee, etc.
bridge *(n)* the raised platform across a ship where the captain and
  officers control the ship
bushel a measurement of grain (about 35 litres)
cab a taxi
cable *(n)* a strong, heavy rope
cargo things carried by a ship
class a group of students taught together
coal a black mineral dug from the ground that is burnt to give
  heat
concrete a building material made of sand, stones, cement and
  water
contract *(n)* a legal agreement, usually in writing
cop *(slang)* a policeman
crane *(n)* a machine with a long moveable arm for lifting heavy
  objects
crumple to push into an irregular shape
crush *(v)* to break by pushing with great force
deadlock a complete failure to reach agreement or solve an
  argument
deck *(n)* the floor of a ship

executor a person who is appointed to carry out the orders in someone's will

expressway a wide road for fast travel

extinguisher something used to put out fires

file *(n)* a box or cover for keeping papers in order

fluid a liquid

footprint the mark made on the ground by a foot

funeral the ceremony of burying a dead person

furious very angry

grab to take hold of something suddenly and roughly

grain the small, hard seed of food plants, e.g. corn, wheat, etc.

grip *(v)* to take and hold something tightly

guy *(informal)* a man

hawk a strong bird that catches small animals for food

hockey a game played with sticks and a small ball

hold *(n)* the place at the bottom of a ship, where cargo is carried

insurance an agreement to pay money in case of accident

Interstate American English for an expressway between states

invoice *(n)* a bill for goods received

licence a paper giving official permission to do something

lock *(n)* an area of water, closed off by gates at each end so that the water level can be raised or lowered

mail *(American English)* to post a letter, card, etc.

mistress a married man's female lover

mourn to show and feel great sadness when someone dies

nod *(v)* to move the head up and down to show agreement

offensive extremely rude or upsetting

photocopy *(v)* to make a photographic copy of something written or printed

picklock a tool for unlocking a door without using a key

port a place where ships load and unload cargo

pulley a wheel with a rope round it, for lifting things
research detailed study to discover new facts or information
satisfy to give somebody what they want, demand, or need
share *(n)* part of a business offered for sale to the public
shatter *(v)* to break suddenly into very small pieces
sherry a strong yellow or brown wine, from Spain
shrug *(v)* to raise the shoulders to show doubt
signal *(n)* an electronic message sent or received
slam *(v)* to push with great force
smart *(adj)* well-dressed; fashionable
stage *(n)* a raised platform on which dancers perform
steel *(adj)* a hard, strong metal made from iron
stowaway a person who hides on a ship to make a free journey
trophy a prize for winning a competition
truck a lorry
trunk *(American English)* the place for luggage at the back of a
  car
vandal a criminal who damages public or private property just
  for fun
vice-president the person who acts for the president
warehouse a large building for storing things
weight the heaviness of something
wharf a place where ships are tied up to load or unload
yacht a sailing boat used especially for racing

Deadlock

ACTIVITIES

Before Reading

1 The title of this book is a play on words. Use the glossary in the book, or a dictionary, and complete these definitions.

deadlock means _____

dead means _____

a lock (on a river or canal) is _____

You have probably guessed that this is a story about murder, but do you think it is connected with:

1 hospitals?   2 ships?   3 banks?   4 hotels?

2 Read the story introduction on the first page of the book, and the back cover. For each sentence, circle Y (Yes) or N (No).

1 Vic Warshawski isn't married. Y/N

2 Vic works for the police. Y/N

3 Vic's cousin is dead. Y/N

4 Vic doesn't believe her cousin's death was an accident. Y/N

5 Vic knew her cousin's girlfriend well. Y/N

3 What do you think will happen in the story? For each sentence, circle Y (Yes) or N (No).

1 Vic will be murdered. Y/N

2 Boom Boom's girlfriend will kill someone. Y/N

3 Vic will find out who killed her cousin. Y/N

4 The murderer will go to prison. Y/N

While Reading

Read Chapters 1–3, and then answer these questions.

1 Why did Vic want to find out more about Boom Boom's death?
2 What did Boom Boom's grandmother tell Vic?
3 What was Paige Carrington doing in Boom Boom's apartment?
4 Who were the four men with Vic at lunch in the club, and what connection did they have with Boom Boom?
5 What was the accident to the *Lucella Wieser*?
6 Why did Grafalk dislike Bledsoe?
7 What did Vic find in the study on her second visit to Boom Boom's apartment?

Read Chapters 4–6. Here are some untrue sentences about them. Change them into true sentences.

1 According to Janet, Boom Boom got on well with Mr Phillips.
2 Bobby Mallory was pleased that Vic was investigating her cousin's death.
3 Bledsoe told Vic that shipping contracts were only cancelled if another company offered a better price.
4 The brakes on Vic's car were damaged but she could still steer it.
5 Howard Mattingly was a good hockey player and a close friend of Boom Boom's.
6 Niels Grafalk's father didn't want Martin Bledsoe to go to prison.

Before you read Chapters 7–10, complete these sentences with the correct names. Which of these people do you think were involved in Boom Boom's death? Why?

1 . . . is vice-president of Eudora Grain.
2 . . . was Boom Boom's secretary.
3 . . . is a policeman.
4 . . . owns the Grafalk Steamship Line.
5 . . . is a newspaper reporter.
6 . . . is a ballet dancer.
7 . . . owns the Pole Star Line.
8 . . . are ice hockey players.

Read Chapters 7–10. Choose the best question-word for these questions and then answer them.

Why / Who / What / How

1 . . . did Vic fly to Thunder Bay?
2 . . . did Vic see in the water when she got on the ship for the second time?
3 . . . did the man with red hair set off the bomb?
4 . . . had Bledsoe's plane already left when Vic arrived at Sault Ste Marie airport?
5 . . . was Vic looking for when she searched the Eudora Grain offices?
6 . . . did Vic find behind the photo?
7 . . . was the difference between the invoice and the shipping contract?
8 . . . was found dead in the hold of Martin Bledsoe's ship?

Before you read Chapters 11–13, have you changed your mind about which characters were involved in Boom Boom's death?

94

Read Chapters 11–13, and then answer these questions.

Why

1 . . . did Paige Carrington and Jeannine Phillips protect each other?
2 . . . didn't Mrs Grafalk like Jeannine Phillips?
3 . . . didn't Grafalk tell Eudora Grain that Phillips was cheating them?
4 . . . did Paige agree to watch Boom Boom for Grafalk?
5 . . . did Vic cut a piece of carpet from Grafalk's boat?
6 . . . did Vic cut her arm?
7 . . . did Vic jump into the water?
8 . . . didn't Grafalk shoot Vic while she was in the water?

Before you read Chapter 14, can you guess the answers to these questions?

1 Will Vic tell the police the truth about what Grafalk did?
2 Will Vic tell Claire Grafalk the truth about what Grafalk did?
3 Will Claire Grafalk be angry about her husband's death?
4 Will Paige be sad that Grafalk is dead?
5 Who will take over the Grafalk Steamship Line?

After Reading

1 How did these people die? Who was responsible? Match these characters with the information, and then write a sentence about each one. For example:

Boom Boom Warshawski was pushed under a ship by Clayton Phillips.

People

Boom Boom Warshawski
the watchman at Boom Boom's apartment
Howard Mattingly
Clayton Phillips
Niels Grafalk

How they died	Person responsible
hit / car	Howard Mattingly
push / ship	Clayton Phillips
explode / boat	Niels Grafalk
break / neck	V. I. Warshawski
shoot / head	

2 Do you agree (A) or disagree (D) with these statements? Explain why.

1 Paige Carrington and Jeannine Phillips didn't kill anyone, so they were innocent of any crime.
2 Paige Carrington and Jeannine Phillips were both equally responsible for what happened to Boom Boom.
3 All the deaths in the story happened because of Jeannine Phillips.

3 Fill in the gaps in this summary of Chapter 7 with words from the story connected with ships.

Vic decided to hide as a _____ on the *Lucella* because she was afraid that _____ Bemis would not want her on board his _____. She knew that she would be able to leave the *Lucella* when the ship stopped at the _____ at Sault Ste Marie. After the _____ of _____ had been loaded into the _____ and the *Lucella* was ready to _____, Vic climbed up the ladder to the _____ and waited until the *Lucella* had pulled away from the _____ and was a couple of kilometres from land. Then she went up to the _____ to talk to Bledsoe.

4 Imagine that you are Murray Ryerson. You are going to interview Vic about the explosion that destroyed the *Lucella*. Decide what questions you are going to ask, for example:

Why were you . . . ?   *What happened . . . ?*
Where exactly . . . ?   *What did you . . . ?*
Do you remember . . . ?

Write an article for your newspaper based on the interview. Begin your article like this.

EXPLOSION AT POE LOCK DESTROYS SHIP

Several people were killed _____

5 Complete the conversation that the president of Ajax Insurance had with Claire Grafalk.

AJAX PRESIDENT: I'm afraid your husband may be responsible for

_____

MRS GRAFALK: But why would he do that?

AJAX PRESIDENT: To stop _____

MRS GRAFALK: But why did he want to do that?

AJAX PRESIDENT: Because _____

MRS GRAFALK: Couldn't he build bigger ships of his own?

AJAX PRESIDENT: No. Because _____

MRS GRAFALK: So how did he keep Grafalk Steamship running?

AJAX PRESIDENT: By using _____

MRS GRAFALK: How did you find out about all this?

AJAX PRESIDENT: Ms Warshawski _____

6 Here is part of the story that Vic told Claire Grafalk. Put these sentences in the right order and then join them together to make a paragraph containing five sentences. Use these linking words and change names to pronouns (*he, his,* etc.) where appropriate.

and / (and) so / because / but / that / when

1 Phillips charged a higher price on the invoices.
2 Boom Boom discovered the truth.
3 Grafalk was responsible for blowing up the Lucella.
4 Phillips's wife wanted to live in a wealthy part of Chicago.
5 Phillips made thousands of dollars for himself.
6 Phillips panicked.
7 Phillips killed Boom Boom.
8 Phillips threatened to tell the police.

9 Vic also discovered what was going on.

10 Grafalk killed Phillips.

11 Phillips put one price in the shipping contracts for Eudora Grain.

12 Clayton Phillips was cheating his bosses at Eudora Grain.

13 Phillips went to Grafalk for help.

7 Do you think Vic was right not to tell the police the truth about Niels Grafalk? Why or why not?

8 Writers of crime stories often use *dead* or *death* in their titles. Do you know of any other examples in English or in your language? Are any of them a play on words, like *Deadlock*?

9 Have you read any other stories, or seen any TV programmes or films, about private investigators, male or female? If so, write a short comparison between Vic Warshawski and one of these other investigators. For example:

Agatha Christie's Miss Marple is another single woman who lives alone, but unlike Vic . . .

ABOUT THE AUTHOR

Sara Paretsky was born in Kansas, USA, in 1947. She studied finance and history at university, and she now lives in Chicago, where her husband recently retired from a physics teaching position at the University of Chicago. She is a full-time writer and is best known for her crime thrillers about V. I. Warshawski, a beautiful woman who works as a private detective. There are now a number of authors writing about female 'private eyes', but she was one of the first and she remains one of the most popular. One of her novels about V. I. won the Silver Dagger Award given by the Crime Writers' Association in 1988.

V. I. Warshawski is unusual because she is a woman who undertakes dangerous investigations and often gets hurt. But she is still interested in clothes and good food. The books are set in Chicago and give a lively picture of the city and its people. V. I.'s father was from a Polish family and her mother was Italian, so readers learn something about the mixture of different nationalities that makes up modern America.

Each book is set against the background of a particular type of business, and Sara Paretsky researches this carefully. For *Deadlock* she travelled on a ship through the Great Lakes.

A film was made about V. I. Warshawski in 1991, starring Kathleen Turner as V. I.

ABOUT BOOKWORMS

OXFORD BOOKWORMS LIBRARY
Classics • True Stories • Fantasy & Horror • Human Interest
Crime & Mystery • Thriller & Adventure

The OXFORD BOOKWORMS LIBRARY offers a wide range of original and adapted stories, both classic and modern, which take learners from elementary to advanced level through six carefully graded language stages:

Stage 1 (400 headwords)	**Stage 4** (1400 headwords)
Stage 2 (700 headwords)	**Stage 5** (1800 headwords)
Stage 3 (1000 headwords)	**Stage 6** (2500 headwords)

More than fifty titles are also available on cassette, and there are many titles at Stages 1 to 4 which are specially recommended for younger learners. In addition to the introductions and activities in each Bookworm, resource material includes photocopiable test worksheets and Teacher's Handbooks, which contain advice on running a class library and using cassettes, and the answers for the activities in the books.

Several other series are linked to the OXFORD BOOKWORMS LIBRARY. They range from highly illustrated readers for young learners, to playscripts, non-fiction readers, and unsimplified texts for advanced learners.

Oxford Bookworms Starters	*Oxford Bookworms Factfiles*
Oxford Bookworms Playscripts	*Oxford Bookworms Collection*

Details of these series and a full list of all titles in the OXFORD BOOKWORMS LIBRARY can be found in the *Oxford English* catalogues. A selection of titles from the OXFORD BOOKWORMS LIBRARY can be found on the next pages.

King's Ransom

ED MCBAIN

Retold by Rosalie Kerr

'Calling all cars, calling all cars. Here's the story on the Smoke Rise kidnapping. The missing boy is eight years old, fair hair, wearing a red sweater. His name is Jeffry Reynolds, son of Charles Reynolds, chauffeur to Douglas King.'

The police at the 87th Precinct hate kidnappers. And these kidnappers are stupid, too. They took the wrong boy – the chauffeur's son instead of the son of the rich tycoon, Douglas King. And they want a ransom of $500,000.

A lot of money. But it's not too much to pay for a little boy's life . . . is it?

The Dead of Jericho

COLIN DEXTER

Retold by Clare West

Chief Inspector Morse is drinking a pint of beer. He is thinking about an attractive woman who lives not far away.

The woman he is thinking of is hanging, dead, from the ceiling of her kitchen. On the floor lies a chair, almost two metres away from the woman's feet.

Chief Inspector Morse finishes his pint, and orders another. Perhaps he will visit Anne, after all. But he is in no particular hurry.

Meanwhile, Anne is still hanging in her kitchen, waiting for the police to come and cut her down. She is in no hurry, either.

Brat Farrar

JOSEPHINE TEY

Retold by Ralph Mowat

'You look exactly like him! You can take the dead boy's place and no one will ever know the difference. You'll be rich for life!'

And so the plan was born. At first Brat Farrar fought against the idea; it was criminal, it was dangerous. But in the end he was persuaded, and a few weeks later Patrick Ashby came back from the dead and went home to inherit the family house and fortune. The Ashby family seemed happy to welcome Patrick home, but Brat soon realized that somewhere there was a time-bomb ticking away, waiting to explode . . .

This Rough Magic

MARY STEWART

Retold by Diane Mowat

The Greek island of Corfu lies like a jewel, green and gold, in the Ionian sea, where dolphins swim in the sparkling blue water. What better place for an out-of-work actress to relax for a few weeks?

But the island is full of danger and mysteries, and Lucy Waring's holiday is far from peaceful. She meets a rude young man, who seems to have something to hide. Then there is a death by drowning, and then another . . .

Heat and Dust

RUTH PRAWER JHABVALA

Retold by Clare West

Heat and dust – these simple, terrible words describe the Indian summer. Year after year, endlessly, it is the same. And everyone who experiences this heat and dust is changed for ever.

We often say, in these modern times, that sexual relationships have changed, for better or for worse. But in this book we see that things have not changed. Whether we look back sixty years, or a hundred and sixty, we see that it is not things that change, but people. And, in the heat and dust of an Indian summer, even people are not very different after all.

American Crime Stories

Retold by John Escott

'Curtis Colt didn't kill that liquor store woman, and that's a fact. It's not right that he should have to ride the lightning – that's what prisoners call dying in the electric chair. Curtis doesn't belong in it, and I can prove it.' But can Curtis's girlfriend prove it? Murder has undoubtedly been done, and if Curtis doesn't ride the lightning for it, then who will?

These seven short stories, by well-known writers such as Dashiel Hammett, Patricia Highsmith, and Nancy Pickard, will keep you on the edge of your seat.